HOLY HORRORS

HOLY HORRORS

AN ILLUSTRATED HISTORY OF RELIGIOUS MURDER AND MADNESS

JAMES A. HAUGHT

Prometheus Books • Buffalo, New York

For Nancy, Joel, Jake, Jeb, and Cass

CONTENTS

INTRODUCTION

In 1766 at Abbeville, France, a teen-age boy was accused of singing irreligious songs, mocking the Virgin Mary, marring a crucifix, and wearing his hat while a religious procession passed. Criticizing the church was punishable by death. The youth, Chevalier de La Barre, was sentenced to have his tongue cut out, his right hand cut off, and to be burned at the stake. The great writer Voltaire attempted to save him. The case was appealed to Parliament in Paris. The clergy demanded death, warning of the dire spread of doubt. Parliament showed mercy by allowing the youth to be decapitated instead of mutilated and burned alive. He was first tortured to extract a fuller confession, then executed on July 1, 1766. His corpse was burned, along with a copy of Voltaire's *Philosophical Dictionary*.

*   *   *

In 1980 at Moradabad, India, a pig caused
hundreds of people to kill each other. The
animal walked through a Muslim holy ground.
Muslims, who think pigs are an embodiment of
Satan, accused Hindus of driving the pig into
the sacred spot. Members of both faiths went
on a rampage, stabbing and clubbing. The pig
riot spread to a dozen cities and left 200 dead.

*   *   *

In the 1500s in Mexico, the Aztec theocracy
sacrificed thousands of people to many gods.
Aztecs believed that the sun would disappear
without the daily "nourishment" of human
hearts ripped from victims on stone altars. To
appease the rain god, priests killed shrieking
children so that their tears might induce rain.
In a rite to the maize goddess, a virgin danced
24 hours, then was killed and skinned; her skin
was then worn by a priest in further dancing.

*   *   *

In the 1980s, Iran's Shi'ite theocracy—"the
government of God on earth"—decreed that

Christians versus Muslims in the Crusades. (Medieval engraving reprinted in *Meyer's Konnerlations-Lexicon,* Leipzig, 1895.)

Baha'i believers who wouldn't convert to Islam must be killed. About 200 Baha'is, including women and teen-agers, were hanged or shot by firing squads. Some 40,000 others fled Iran.

*   *   *

In 1583 at Vienna, a 16-year-old girl suffered stomach cramps. A team of Jesuits exorcized her for eight weeks. The priests announced that they had expelled 12,652 demons from her, demons her grandmother had kept as flies in glass jars. The grandmother was tortured into confessing she was a witch who had engaged in sex with Satan. Then she was burned at the stake. This was one of perhaps 1 million such executions during three centuries of witch-hunts.

*   *   *

In 1983 at Darkley, Northern Ireland, Catholic terrorists with automatic weapons burst into a Protestant church on a Sunday morning and opened fire, killing three worshipers and wounding seven. It was one of hundreds of Protestant-Catholic ambushes, which have cost nearly 3,000 lives during twenty years of religious conflict in Northern Ireland.

An Anabaptist being burned alive at Amsterdam in 1571 for the offense of believing in double baptism. (One of many copper engravings by Dutch artist Jan Luyken in the 1685 edition of *Martyrs Mirror*, reprinted by courtesy of Lancaster Mennonite Historical Society.)

*   *   *

In 1096, at the start of the First Crusade,
thousands of Christians massed into legions to
march to the Holy Land to destroy infidels. In
Germany, some Crusaders followed a goose
they believed to be enchanted by God. It led
them into Jewish neighborhoods, where they
hacked and burned the residents to death.

*   *   *

"Men never do evil so completely and
cheerfully as when they do it from religious
conviction," philosopher Blaise Pascal wrote.

Jonathan Swift, looking back over centuries
of church carnage, made his famous comment:
"We have just enough religion to make us hate,
but not enough to make us love one another."

Thomas Jefferson, in his *Notes on Virginia*,
wrote:

"Millions of innocent men, women, and
children, since the introduction of Christianity,
have been burned, tortured, fined, and
imprisoned, yet we have not advanced one inch
toward uniformity. What has been the effect of
coercion? To make one half of the world fools
and the other half hypócrites."

Aztec priests offer a sacrifice victim's heart to the sun god. (From the Florentine Codex created by Aztec Indian artists, circa 1550. American Museum of Natural History.)

But Christianity has no monopoly on killing for God. Even before the birth of Christ, the Roman poet Lucretius warned: "How many evils have flowed from religion!"

A grim pattern is visible in history: When religion is the ruling force in a society, it produces horror. The stronger the supernatural beliefs, the worse the inhumanity. A culture dominated by intense faith invariably is cruel to people who don't share the faith—and sometimes to many who do.

When religion was all-powerful in Europe, it produced the epic bloodbath of the Crusades, the torture chambers of the Inquisition, mass extermination of "heretics," hundreds of massacres of Jews, and 300 years of witch-burnings. The split of the Reformation loosed a torrent of hate that took millions of lives in a dozen religious wars. The "Age of Faith" was an age of holy slaughter. When religion gradually ceased to control daily life, the concept of human rights and personal freedoms took root.

Today, much of the Third World hasn't broken free from religious horror. In India, Sikhs, Hindus, and Muslims repeatedly massacre each other. In Iran, Shi'ite fundamentalists subjugate women and kill

Polish Protestants were crushed in the early 1600s under ardent Catholic King Sigismund III, nicknamed "the King of the Jesuits." (From *Martyrs Mirror*, 1685, courtesy of Lancaster Mennonite Historical Society.)

"blasphemers." In Lebanon, Sunnis, Shi'ites, Druzes, Maronites, and Alawites destroy their nation and themselves. In Sri Lanka, Buddhists and Hindus exchange atrocities. In the Sudan, Muslims, Christians, and animists slaughter each other. It's fashionable among thinking people to say that religion isn't the real cause of these modern nightmares, that it merely provides labels for warring factions. Not so. Faith keeps the groups apart, alienated in hostile camps. "Religious tribalism" sets the stage for bloodshed. Without it, young people might adapt to changing times, intermarry, and forget historic wounds. But religion enforces separation—and whatever separates people breeds conflict.

Paradoxically, in spite of its gory record, religion is almost universally deemed a power for good, a generator of compassion. Former President Ronald Reagan called it "the bedrock of moral order." President George Bush said it gives people "the character they need to get through life."

Obviously, religion has a Jekyll-and-Hyde nature—with Dr. Jekyll always in the spotlight, and Mr. Hyde little noticed. Modern Westerners, accustomed to free lives in secular society, have largely forgotten the monster

16

lurking behind supernatural beliefs. Europeans and Americans were startled in 1989 when Iran's Ayatollah Khomeini ordered religious assassination of a "blaspheming" British author who had hinted that Mohammed's pronouncements weren't dictated by Allah. The wave of surprise showed how little the West remembers about religion.

At the height of the international crisis caused by the murder decree, scholars held an "Anatomy of Hate" conference at Boston University. Participants included a daughter of former Egyptian President Anwar Sadat, who was killed by Islamic fundamentalists who felt he had betrayed the faith. Harvard theologian Krister Stendahl commented: "Religion is a very dangerous thing. These are enormous powers we are dealing with. . . . Why has there been this dark side?"

This book traces the dark and dangerous side of religion through the past nine centuries.

THE CRUSADES

Through the haze of legend, the Crusades are remembered as a romantic quest by noble knights wearing crimson crosses. In reality, the Crusades were a sickening nightmare of slaughter, rape, looting, and chaos—mixed with belief in magic. The crusaders killed nearly as many Christians and Jews as they did Muslims, their intended target.

Pope Urban II launched the First Crusade in 1095 to wrest the Holy Land from infidels. "Deus Vult" (God wills it) became the rallying cry. Around Europe, masses of zealots swarmed into mob-type armies led by charismatic priests. Tens of thousands followed an unwashed priest, Peter the Hermit, who displayed a letter he said was written to him by God and delivered to him by Jesus as his credentials for leadership. Other thousands followed a priest called Walter the Penniless.

In the Rhine Valley of Germany, one throng of crusaders followed a goose they thought had been enchanted by God to be their guide. This group joined the army of Emich of Leisingen, a leader who said a cross miraculously had appeared on his chest as a holy sign. Emich's multitude decided that, before marching 2,000 miles to kill God's enemies in Israel, their first religious duty was to slay "the infidels among us," the Jews of Mainz, Worms, and other German cities. They swept in unstoppable waves through Jewish quarters, chopping and burning thousands of defenseless men, women, and children. Many Jews, trapped and doomed in barricaded quarters, tearfully killed their children and themselves before the mob broke in.

Similar hordes led by priests Volkmar and Gottschalk likewise massacred Jews of Prague and Regensburg, Bavaria. Occasionally, victims were given a last-minute opportunity, at swordpoint, to save their lives by converting to Christianity.

As the various peasant armies moved through Christian Hungary, Yugoslavia, and Bulgaria, they pillaged the countryside for food,

Christian crusaders catapulted Muslim heads into the besieged cities of Antioch, Nicea, and Tyre. (Illumination from *Les Histoires d'Outremer* by William of Tyre, 13th century. Bibliothèque Nationale, Paris.)

provoking battles with local peoples and armies. In one clash, Peter the Hermit's army killed 4,000 Christian residents of Zemun, Yugoslavia, then burned nearby Belgrade. In turn, thousands of crusaders died in confused fighting in Bulgaria. Only a fraction of the peasant mobs finally reached Muslim Turkey, where they soon were exterminated by Turkish armies.

Organized regiments of Christian knights followed the rabble, bringing professionalism to the Crusade. Accompanying bishops blessed their atrocities. The advancing legions decapitated Muslims and carried the heads as trophies. During three sieges—at Nicea, Antioch, and Tyre—crusaders catapulted Muslim heads into the surrounded cities to demoralize defenders. After a victory on the Syrian coast near Antioch, Frankish crusaders brought 500 heads back to camp. Three hundred of them were put on stakes before the city to torment defenders atop the walls. Chronicler-priests recorded that a crusader bishop called the impaled heads a joyful spectacle for the people of God. The other 200 heads were catapulted into Antioch. Inside, Muslims decapitated Antioch's Christian residents and catapulted *their* heads outward in

Severed heads, hands, and legs dot this scene of Christian-Muslim warfare. (Medieval manuscript illumination.)

a grotesque crossfire. The crusaders finally broke through on June 3, 1098, and slaughtered inhabitants.

Then an arriving Muslim army encircled Antioch and besieged the former besiegers. The Franks were near starvation when one Peter Bartholomew announced that a saint had appeared to him in a vision and disclosed that the lance that pierced Christ's side at the crucifixion was buried beneath a Christian church in Antioch. The Holy Lance was dug up and became a miraculous relic inspiring the crusaders to ferocity. They stormed out of the city in a fanatical onslaught that sent the Muslim soldiers fleeing in panic, abandoning their camp—and their wives. Chronicler Fulcher of Chartres proudly recorded: "When their women were found in the tents, the Franks did nothing evil to them except pierce their bellies with their lances."

(Whether the Holy Lance was genuine or a planted fake wasn't questioned by the crusade's chronicler-priests. Christendom was obsessed with finding and worshiping sacred relics, alleged evidence from Bible stories. Fragments of "the true cross," pieces of saints' bodies, still-wet tears shed by Jesus, barbs from the Crown of Thorns, Mary's undergarments—such were treasured in jeweled cases in every major church. A ruler of Saxony proudly possessed 17,000 relics, including a branch from Moses's burning bush and a feather from the wings of the Angel Gabriel. Canterbury Cathedral displayed part of the clay left over after God fashioned Adam. Historian Charles Mackay said Spanish churches had six or seven thighbones of the Virgin Mary, and others had enough of St. Peter's toenails to fill a sack. Voltaire noted that six sacred foreskins were snipped from Jesus at his circumcision; later researchers counted fifteen.)

Marching on to Jerusalem, the crusaders soon topped the walls and "purified" the symbolic city by slaughtering virtually every resident. Jews who took shelter in their synagogue were burned alive. Corpses were piled in the streets. Chronicler Raymond of Aguilers recorded:

"Wonderful things were to be seen. Numbers of the Saracens were beheaded. . . . Others were shot with arrows, or forced to jump from the towers; others were tortured for several days, then burned in flames. In the streets were seen piles of heads and hands and feet. One rode about everywhere amid the corpses of men and horses. . . .

"In the temple of Solomon, the horses waded in blood up to their knees, nay, up to the bridle. It was a just and marvelous judgment of God, that this place should be filled with the blood of the unbelievers."

During the subsequent two centuries, Muslim recaptures of portions of the Holy Land caused seven other Christian crusades. Most of these expeditions began, as the first had, with massacres of Jews at home.

In the Third Crusade, after Richard the Lion-Hearted captured Acre in 1191, he ordered 3,000 captives—many of them women and children—taken outside the city and massacred. The corpses were cut open in a search for swallowed gems. Bishops intoned blessings. Chronicler Ambroise wrote: "They were slaughtered every one. For this be the Creator blessed!" Infidel lives were of no consequence. As St. Bernard of Clairvaux had declared in launching the Second Crusade: "The Christian glories in the death of a pagan, because thereby Christ himself is glorified."

In the Fourth Crusade, the armies became diverted and sacked the Christian cities of Constantinople and Zara. The Children's Crusade in 1212 was a tragedy based on the mistaken belief that God would empower innocent Christian tots to overwhelm Muslim armies. Most of the children perished without reaching the Holy Land.

Finally, it all came to an end in 1291 when Muslims recaptured the last Christian stronghold, Acre, and slaughtered its garrison in retaliation for Richard's massacre a century earlier. The Holy Land was back in Muslim hands. Two centuries of death and destruction had been for nothing.

Subsequent popes attempted to rouse armies for further crusades, but few legions responded. A final spasm occurred three centuries later, after Muslims had captured Constantinople. Pope Pius V decreed a crusade, and Christian kings supplied a naval armada commanded by Don Juan of Austria. French historian Henry Daniel-Rops recounted:

"On October 7, 1571, Christ's warriors, chanting the psalms, gave battle in the Gulf of Lepanto. It was a terrible engagement, full of surprises and anxiety. Don Juan himself stood on the prow of his flagship, holding a crucifix. When evening fell over the glorious bay, the smoke of burning Turkish galleys spread a reek of timber and corpses. The entire enemy fleet had been destroyed or captured, and aboard the *Marquesa* a wounded soldier named Miguel de

Cervantes, whose arm had been shattered in the fight, joined in the *Te Deum*."

HUMAN SACRIFICE

It boggles the modern mind to realize that, in some past cultures dominated by religion and priests, people sent their children to be strangled, beheaded, burned, drowned, skinned, crushed, and otherwise killed as appeasement offerings to gods now known to be imaginary.

Human sacrifice seems insane in retrospect, but it was routine to people taught endlessly to dread feathered-serpent gods, invisible crop gods, unseen goddesses of destruction, and the like. The slaughter wasn't confined to Old Testament times, but reached a heyday relatively recently in the elaborate Mayan, Incan, and Aztec societies of Latin America and the Thuggee cult of India.

Over the centuries, sacrifice had many varieties. In ancient Phoenicia, boys were burned to satisfy Adonis and other gods—and the fall of Carthage was blamed on the faithlessness of nobles who substituted children of slaves for their own on the altars. In ancient Gaul, the Druids allegedly put victims into large wicker figures of men and set them afire. In Tibet, Bon shamans performed ritual killing. In Africa, the Ashanti offered about 100 victims each September to assure a good yam harvest. In Borneo, builders of pile-houses drove the first pile though the body of a maiden to pacify the earth goddess.

The golden age of sacrifice came with highly organized theocracies in Central America. After the Mayans amalgamated with fierce neighbor tribes in the 11th century, ritual killings proliferated to appease the plumed serpent Kukulcan (later called Quetzalcoatl by the Aztecs) and sundry other gods. Maidens were drowned in sacred wells, and other victims were beheaded, shot with arrows, or had their hearts cut out.

In Peru, pre-Inca tribes killed children in "houses of the moon." Beginning in the 1200s, the Incas built a complex theocracy dominated by priests who read daily magical signs and offered sacrifices to many gods. At major ceremonies, up to 200 children were burned as

Sacrifice victim's heart seems to leap into the sky in this Indian drawing of an Aztec sacrifice. (From the Codex Magliabechiano. Library of Congress print collection.)

offerings. Mothers brought their darlings dressed in finery and flowers to be put to death. Special "chosen women"—comely virgins without blemish—sometimes were removed from their temple duties and strangled. Local rulers sent choice daughters to the capital at Cuzco as chosen women. Later they were sent back to be buried alive.

The ultimate murder religion was that of the Aztecs, which demanded about 20,000 victims per year. The chief deity was the sun, which might disappear, priests warned, without daily sustenance of hearts and blood. Multitudes of victims, mostly prisoners of war, were held on stone altars by clergy who ripped out their hearts with obsidian knives. Flesh from their arms was eaten ritually, and their skulls were preserved on racks holding as many as 10,000 heads. Raids called "wars of the flowers" were conducted to seize plentiful sacrifice candidates.

Priests also killed many Aztecs. Weeping children were sacrificed so that their tears might induce the rain god to water the crops. To please the maize goddess, dancing virgins were seized, decapitated, and skinned—and their skins were worn by priests in continued dancing.

In 1487, when the great Aztec temple in Tenochtitlan was dedicated, eight teams of priests worked four days sacrificing 20,000 prisoners, the entire manpower of three captured tribes.

This classic era of sacrifice ended when conquering Spaniards destroyed the Mayan, Incan, and Aztec civilizations. The Spanish forcibly converted most of these peoples to Christianity—occasionally burning backsliders—but traces of the old gods and sacrifice lingered. As late as 1868 an Indian boy was sacrificed in Chiapas.

In the Far East, five different types of human sacrifice were halted by British rulers in the 1800s. One was the yearly *meriah* by the Khonds of Bengal, who cut a victim into small pieces and buried the fragments in many fields to assure a good harvest. Another was a weekly rite by certain followers of the bloodthirsty Hindu goddess Kali who sacrificed a male child every Friday evening at a shrine in Tanjore, India.

A third was the Hindu code of suttee, which required a widow to leap onto her dead husband's funeral pyre, willingly or unwillingly. The British banned it in 1829, but it persisted. (When Brahmans of Sind protested that suttee

was their holy custom, Governor Charles
Napier replied: "My nation also has a custom:
When men burn women alive, we hang them.
Let us all act according to national customs.")

In Burma, the Buddhist king moved the
capital to Mandalay in 1854 and sanctified the
new city walls by burying scores of "spotless"
men alive in vats under the gates and bastions.
In 1861, two of the vats were discovered to be
empty—whereupon royal astrologers declared
that 500 men, women, boys, and girls must be
killed and buried at once, or the capital must be
abandoned. About 100 actually were buried
before British authorities stopped the
ceremonies.

The worst holy slaughter halted by the
British was the infamous Thuggee strangling in
India. For generations, certain secretive
followers of Kali, the goddess of destruction,
had been ritually dispatching an estimated
20,000 victims a year. The toll since the 1500s
was estimated as high as 2 million. Thug
theology held that Brahma the Creator
produced new lives faster than Shiva the
Destroyer could end them, so Shiva's wife Kali
commanded believers to hunt humans and
garrote them with sashes.

Thugs usually preyed upon travelers in

unpopulated places. Victims were seized, strangled, ceremonially gashed, and buried—then the Thugs ate a ritual meal over the burial spot. (They also plundered the victim's possessions—another motive for their religious fervor.) British officers finally broke Thuggee by ferreting out 3,689 cultists and hanging or imprisoning them, or branding them with "Thug" as a public warning. At a trial in 1840, one Thug was accused of strangling 931 people.

Other sacrifices lingered. In the 1800s an Ashanti king in Africa, wishing to make his new palace impregnable, sacrificed 200 girls and mixed their blood in the mortar of the walls. In 1838 a Pawnee American Indian girl was cut to pieces to fertilize newly sown crops. During the late 1800s, bodies of sacrificed children occasionally were found at Kali shrines in India. During a Russian famine in the 1890s, a dozen Votiaks were sentenced to life imprisonment for hanging a victim upside down in a tree and tearing out his heart to appease the earth god Kourbane.

ISLAMIC JIHADS

Waging bloody warfare as a means to spread a religion espousing compassion may seem contradictory, yet that's how the world's second-largest faith grew. And, after it grew, it split into hostile segments waging holy wars against each other.

Combat was part of Islam from its beginning. The prophet Mohammed conquered Mecca by force. He fought in nine battles and ordered several others. He dictated the Koran, which sanctions armed *jihads* as a tool of evangelism. (It also authorizes nonviolent jihads by heart, tongue, and hand.)

The new faith unified the fierce Bedou tribes of the Arabian peninsula, who had spent centuries in cruel tribal warfare. They became the shock troops of wars for Islam. Immediately after Mohammed's death in 632, successor caliphs launched a seemingly endless series of holy wars—first against apostate tribes who seceded when the prophet died, then against neighboring nations. Fanatical Bedou armies leaped out of Arabia onto an unsuspecting world. They rapidly conquered Syria, Iraq, Palestine, Egypt, and Persia. Then the holy war was pressed eastward to India and westward through North Africa and Spain, finally being halted in 732 in a decisive battle at Tours, France.

Meanwhile, constant assassinations and rebellions erupted among the faithful. Shi'ite followers of Mohammed's son-in-law Ali fought doomed wars against the Sunni majority. The Kharijis, a splinter of Shi'ites, fought savagely for centuries as puritanical terrorists until they became nearly extinct. The ultra-fanatical Azariqis decreed death to all "sinners" and their families.

A strange variation of holy war was waged by the Assassins, a small Ismaili sect that disagreed violently with Sunni caliphs in the 1100s and 1200s. Too few for direct warfare, the Assassins sent lone killers in disguise to inveigle their way into the presence of Sunni leaders and stab them—usually a suicide mission.

A London newspaper's view of the jihad in the Nile valley in the 1890s. (From *The Graphic*, Feb. 2, 1885.)

The Assassins operated from a string of mountain strongholds in Iran and Iraq. Members were zealots willing to accept martyrdom to accomplish their murder missions. One visitor to an Assassin castle reported that the leader, "the old man of the mountains," demonstrated his followers' obedience by ordering a white-robed guard to leap off a castle wall. The guard saluted and plunged to his death. Marco Polo and others wrote that hashish was given to members to induce their unthinking actions—but no hard evidence supports this.

Decade after decade, the Assassins killed holy men, Sunni statesmen, generals—even two caliphs. Muslim leaders had to wear armor under their robes when they went to mosques or public places. During the Crusades, Assassins made two attempts on the life of Muslim chieftain Saladin, and they killed Christian commander Conrad de Montferrat. Finally, campaigns by Mongols and sultans destroyed the Assassins—leaving their name as an appropriate legacy.

Beginning in the 1700s, a new wave of jihads flared. In the Arabian peninsula, Mohammed al-Wahhab preached that Islam had been corrupted by worldly frills and must be cleansed by fire. He declared war on "the infidel," fellow Muslims. After his death, his Wahhabi Bedou army conquered several cities in the early 1800s, massacring residents. This drew counterattacks by Turks and Egyptians, who drove the "heretics" into the desert, captured their leaders, and beheaded them. After a century of ferment, Wahhabis rose again in the early 1900s as fanatical "brothers," conquering the peninsula and creating the modern kingdom of Saudi Arabia.

"From 1745 to 1934," historian Daniel Pipes wrote, "virtually every battle the Wahhabis fought was against Muslim enemies. . . . The Wahhabis genuinely considered other Muslims untrue to the faith and therefore proper objects of jihad. Religious differences motivated these wars."

In 1804, a Nigerian holy man, Usman dan Fodio, declared a jihad against the Sultan of Gobir. Four years of fighting killed thousands and toppled the sultan.

In 1854, in what is now the African Republic of Mali, holy man 'Umar al-Hajj declared a jihad against pagan Africans and Muslim Fulani people. Leading an army of 10,000, he terrorized the region, beheading opponents and executing 300 hostages at one time. 'Umar finally was defeated, driven into a cave, and killed by a gunpowder blast.

In the 1880s, in the Nile regions of Sudan, holy man Muhammad Ahmad proclaimed himself the prophesied Mahdi (divinely guided one) and declared a jihad against "the faithless ones." His legions destroyed a 10,000-man Egyptian army, then massacred defenders of Khartoum, including British General "Chinese" Gordon. The Mahdi died and his successor attempted to wage a holy war against all of Islam. But British-Egyptian armies crushed him. One force under Sir Herbert Kitchener (and a young officer named Winston Churchill) used Maxim guns to mow down 20,000 Mahdists in a single day.

BLOOD LIBEL

Century after century, the Catholic church
preached that Jews were "Christ-killers." St.
Gregory called them "slayers of the Lord,
murderers of the prophets, adversaries of
God." St. Jerome added "vipers" and "cursers of
Christians." St. Bernard of Clairvaux called
them "a degraded and perfidious people." When
a bishop burned a synagogue at Callinicum, St.
Ambrose wrote: "Who cares if a synagogue—
home of insanity and unbelief—is destroyed?"
St. John Chrysostom wrote:

"The Jews sacrifice their children to Satan.
. . . They are worse than wild beasts. . . . The
synagogue is a brothel, a den of scoundrels, the
temple of demons devoted to idolatrous cults, a
criminal assembly of Jews, a place of meeting
for the assassins of Christ."

Liturgical chants cited "the perfidious Jews." Passion plays depicted them cruelly mocking Jesus. The message had effect. Anti-Semitism became an adjunct of Christianity. Jews were clannish, separate, which fueled superstitious suspicions about them. Under such conditions, it's little wonder that scare stories spread.

In 1144 a 12-year-old boy named William was found dead near Norwich, England. Rumor spread that Jews had sacrificed him and used his blood in heinous rituals. A monk, Thomas of Monmouth, wrote a lurid account alleging that Jews routinely sacrificed Christian children. The tale spread like wildfire. A church to the martyr St. William was built at Norwich, becoming a site of pilgrimages and miracles.

Rapidly, the "blood libel" spread over Europe. In city after city, Jews were seized and killed as child-sacrificers. Examples:

In 1171 at Blois, France, thirty-eight Jewish leaders were sentenced to death because the mayor's servant thought he saw a Jew throw a child's body into the river—even though no body was found and no child was missing. The thirty-eight were given a chance to save their lives by converting to Christianity, but they refused. They were locked in a wooden shed, which was burned.

Burning of the Jews of Trent, Italy, in 1475 on allegations that they had sacrificed Christian children. The odd-shaped hats were an identifying badge the Catholic church forced all Jews to wear. (German woodcut widely distributed in the 15th century.)

In 1255 at Lincoln, England, the body of an 8-year-old boy named Hugh was found in the well of a Jew. Hysteria spread. Chronicler Matthew Paris wrote that "the child was first fattened for 10 days with white bread and milk and then almost all the Jews of England were invited to the crucifixion." Jews desperately denied the monstrous accusation—to no avail. Eighteen were tortured and hanged as sacrificers. Little St. Hugh of Lincoln was revered at a shrine built to his memory.

In 1285 at Munich, 180 Jews were burned after a rumor spread that they bled a Christian child to death in their synagogue.

In 1294 at Bern, Switzerland, all Jews were killed or expelled because of a ritual-murder tale. Later, Bern erected "the fountain of the child-devourer," showing an evil-looking Jew holding a sackful of infants and swallowing one of them.

In 1475 at Trent, Italy, reports said a toddler named Simon had been sacrificed. Nearly all Jews of the city were tortured, tried, and burned. Lurid woodcuts portray the events. Simon of Trent was beatified as a Catholic martyr, his feast day was celebrated yearly, and many miracles were reported at his shrine in Trent.

In 1491, Jews being tortured by the Holy Inquisition in Spain were made to confess that they had sacrificed a Christian child in a cave near a village called La Guardia. They were burned, and all Jews in their community were murdered. "The holy child of La Guardia" became a religious legend—yet no such town, or sacrificed child, had existed.

In 1759 a Vatican investigative commission concluded that no Jews ever sacrificed any children: The tales were mere myth.

But the blood libel persisted. In 1801 at Bucharest, Romania, Orthodox priests revived the accusation of ritual blood-drinking. Christians stormed the Jewish quarter and cut the throats of 128 people.

In the late 1800s, Orthodox monks in czarist Russia told of secret sacrifices, stirring hate that helped fuel later pogroms. In 1934, the German Nazi paper *Der Stürmer* inflamed passions by publishing a ghastly illustrated edition depicting Jews draining blood from the throats of innocent blonde children. In 1965 the Vatican finally ordered a halt to the "cult" of Simon of Trent. This was shortly after liberal Pope John XXIII ended church chants about "the perfidious Jews."

HOST-NAILING

The Fourth Lateran Council in 1215 commanded that all Jews in Catholic lands must wear distinguishing labels or garments—a badge of shame similar to the yellow star later imposed by 20th century Nazis. This, plus Vatican orders confining Jews to ghettos, ostracized them as a hated class.

But a different action of the 1215 council inadvertently led to worse consequences for Jews. This action was the passage of the doctrine of transubstantiation: that the host wafer miraculously turns into the body of Jesus during the mass.

Soon, among superstitious people, rumors spread that Jews were stealing the sacred wafers and mutilating them or driving nails through them, to crucify Jesus again. Reports said the pierced host bled, or cried out, or emitted spirits, or turned into a dove or an angel and flew away.

On this charge, Jews were burned at the stake in 1243 in Belitz, Germany—the first of more than a hundred slaughters.

In 1298, a priest spread the host-nailing story in Nuremberg, and 628 Jews were killed, including Mordecai ben Hillel, the famous scholar. That same year, a Bavarian knight named Rindfliesch led an armed brigade that stormed through defenseless Jewish towns to avenge the tortured host. He exterminated 146 communities in six months.

In 1337 at Deggendorf, Bavaria, the entire Jewish population, including children, was burned after stories of host-defiling spread. In the Catholic church, a display of sixteen oil paintings was created, showing Jews mutilating wafers with hammers, thorns, and fire. Priests attached explanatory signs like this one: "The Holy Host is being scraped to the very blood by wicked Jews." For centuries, as many as 10,000 pilgrims came to the church yearly to view the gallery. The practice continued through the 1960s.

In 1370 at Brussels, someone reported seeing a Jew break a wafer, and virtually all

Two panels from a German broadsheet printed in 1480, describing events two years earlier in Passau, Bavaria. Jews were accused of stabbing a stolen host wafer, making it bleed, and were beheaded for it.

Belgian Jews were massacred. One report said 100 were burned, and another said "500 Jews were dragged through the streets of Brussels and, without distinction of sex or age, mutilated until dead." In the cathedral, eighteen tableaux were painted, showing Jews nailing wafers, some of which bled. The display remained until recent times.

Host-desecration rumors and massacres continued randomly in Catholic lands. In 1453 at Breslau, a woman alleged that a Jew stabbed a wafer, and forty-one were burned to death. In 1492 at Mecklenburg, Jews were tortured until they "confessed" to host-defilement, and twenty-seven were burned. In 1510 at Spandau, a tortured Jew "confessed" that he made a wafer bleed and sent it to rabbis of the region. This caused thirty-eight to be burned at Berlin.

As late as 1761, Jews were executed at Nancy, France, on the utterly imaginary allegations.

KILLING HERETICS

Christians killed Muslims in the Crusades.
Christians killed Jews in many massacres.
Meanwhile, another dimension was added:
Christians began killing fellow Christians as
"heretics."

During the first millenium of the church,
execution for doctrinal deviation was rare. In
A.D. 385 at Trier, Germany, bishops put to
death Priscillian and his followers for doubting
the Trinity and the Resurrection. At Alexandria
in 415, the great woman scientist Hypatia, head
of the Alexandria Library, was beaten to death
by monks and other followers of St. Cyril, who
viewed her science much as the church later
viewed Galileo's. At Constantinople around 550,
the Byzantine Emperor Justinian killed
multitudes of non-conformists to impose

Christian orthodoxy. Otherwise, heresy was a minor issue.

After the turn of the millenium, a few prosecutions occurred. King Robert the Pious burned thirteen heretics at Orleans in 1022. At Goslar, Germany, a community of Christians— deviants whose beliefs made them unwilling to kill chickens—were convicted of heresy and hanged in 1051. In 1141, priest Peter Abelard was sentenced to life imprisonment because he listed church contradictions in a book titled *Yes and No.*

Then, in the 1200s, a storm of heretic-hunting burst upon Europe. The first victims were the Albigenses, or Cathari, centered around Albi, France. They doubted the biblical account of Creation, considered Jesus an angel instead of a god, rejected transubstantiation, and demanded strict celibacy. Bishops executed a few Albigenses leaders, but the sect continued growing. The Third Lateran Council in 1179 proclaimed a military crusade against them, but it was a minor expedition with little success.

In 1208, Pope Innocent III declared a major crusade to destroy the Albigenses. Some 20,000 knights and peasants answered the call, forming an army that scourged southern

Albigenses Christians, also called Cathari and Publicani, were burned by Catholic bishops in the late 1100s, before the pope declared a military crusade against them. (From *Martyrs Mirror*, 1685, courtesy of Lancaster Mennonite Historical Society.)

France, smashing towns where the belief was strong. When the besieged city of Beziers fell, soldiers asked papal legate Arnald Amalric (or Arnaud Amaury) how they could distinguish the infidel from the faithful among the captives. He commanded: "Kill them all. God will know His own." Thousands were slaughtered—many first blinded, mutilated, dragged behind horses or used for target practice. The legate reported to the pope: "God's wrath has raged in wondrous wise against the city."

This was the beginning of numerous "internal crusades" against nonconforming Christians and rebellious lords.

Another group targeted for extermination were the Waldensians, followers of Peter Waldo of Lyon, lay preachers who sermonized in the streets. The church decreed that only priests could preach, and commanded them to cease. They persisted. The Waldensians had been excommunicated as heretics at the Council of Verona in 1184, and the Albigensian crusade was directed at them as well. Executions ensued for five centuries. The lay preachers fled to Germany and Italy, where they frequently were caught and burned. Some hid in caves. In 1487, Pope Innocent VIII

About 2,000 Waldensian Protestants in Calabria, southern Italy, were massacred in 1560 by Catholic troops under Grand Inquisitor Michele Ghislieri, who later became Pope Pius V and was sainted. (Library of Congress print collection.)

declared an armed crusade against Waldensians in the Savoy region of France.

Also condemned were the Amalricans. French theologian Amalric of Bena preached that all people are potentially divine, and that church rites aren't needed. After his death in the 1200s, his followers were burned alive as heretics, and his body was dug up and burned.

A similar fate befell the Apostolic Brethren, who preached and sang in public. Leader Gerhard Segarelli was burned as a heretic in 1300. His successor, Dolcino, led survivors into fortified places to withstand attacks and wage counterattacks. Troops of the bishop of Milan overran their fort and killed nearly all of them. Dolcino was burned in 1307.

In 1318 a group of Celestine or "Spiritual" Franciscan monks were burned because they refused to abandon the primitive simplicity of Franciscan garb and manners. Others executed as heretics included Beghards and Beguines, who lived in Christian communes, and the Brothers of the Free Spirit, a mystical order of monks.

The Knights Templar, religious warriors of an order that originated in the Crusades, were accused in France in 1307 of spitting on crucifixes and worshiping the devil. They were subjected to extreme torture, which killed some of them; others "confessed." About seventy were burned at the stake.

Killing heretics was endorsed by popes and saints. They quoted Old Testament mandates such as "He who blasphemes the name of the Lord shall be put to death." St. Thomas Aquinas declared: "If coiners and other malefactors are justly doomed to death, much more may heretics be justly slain."

THE INQUISITION

Efforts to stamp out heresy led to the establishment of the Holy Inquisition, one of mankind's supreme horrors. In the early 1200s, local bishops were empowered to identify, try, and punish heretics. When the bishops proved ineffective, traveling papal inquisitors, usually Dominican priests, were sent from Rome to conduct the purge.

Pope Innocent IV authorized torture in 1252, and the Inquisition chambers became places of terror. Accused heretics were seized and locked in cells, unable to see their families, unable to know the names of their accusers. If they didn't confess quickly, unspeakable cruelties began. Swiss historian Walter Nigg recounted:

"The thumbscrew was usually the first to

be applied: The fingers were placed in clamps and the screws turned until the blood spurted out and the bones were crushed. The defendant might be placed on the iron torture chair, the seat of which consisted of sharpened iron nails that could be heated red-hot from below. There were the so-called 'boots,' which were employed to crush the shinbones. Another favorite torture was dislocation of the limbs on the rack or the wheel on which the heretic, bound hand and foot, was drawn up and down while the body was weighted with stones.

"So that the torturers would not be disturbed by the shrieking of the victim, his mouth was stuffed with cloth. Three- and four-hour sessions of torture were nothing unusual. During the procedure the instruments were frequently sprinkled with holy water."

The victim was required not only to confess that he was a heretic, but also to accuse his children, wife, friends, and others as fellow heretics, so that they might be subjected to the same process. Minor offenders and those who confessed immediately received lighter sentences. Serious heretics who repented were given life imprisonment and their possessions were confiscated. Others were led to the stake

St. Dominic wears a halo in this church painting as he presides over an Inquisition session deciding the fate of two accused heretics stripped and bound to posts at lower right. (By Pedro Berruguete, circa 1500. Prado Museum, Madrid.)

in a procession and church ceremony called the "auto-da-fé" (act of the faith). A papal statute of 1231 decreed burning as the standard penalty. The actual executions were performed by civil officers, not priests, as a way of preserving the church's sanctity.

Some inquisitors cut terrible swaths. Robert le Bourge sent 183 to the stake in a single week. Bernard Gui convicted 930—confiscating the property of all 930, sending 307 to prison, and burning forty-two. Conrad of Marburg burned every suspect who claimed innocence. He met his downfall when he accused a count of riding on a crab in a diabolical rite, whereupon an archbishop declared the charge groundless and Conrad was murdered, presumably by agents of the count.

Historically, the Inquisition is divided into three phases: the medieval extermination of heretics; the Spanish Inquisition in the 1400s; and the Roman Inquisition, which began after the Reformation.

In Spain, thousands of Jews had converted to Christianity to escape death in recurring Christian massacres. So, too, had some Muslims. They were, however, suspected of being insincere converts clandestinely practicing their old religion. In 1478 the pope

Pope Pius V and his cardinals (background) watch the Roman Inquisition burn a nonconforming religious scholar, about 1570. Pius later was canonized a saint. (From *Harper's* magazine in the 1800s.)

authorized King Ferdinand and Queen Isabella to revive the Inquisition to hunt "secret Jews" and their Muslim counterparts. Dominican friar Tomas de Torquemada was appointed inquisitor general, and he became a symbol of religious cruelty. Thousands upon thousands of screaming victims were tortured, and at least 2,000 were burned.

The Roman period began in 1542 when Pope Paul III sought to eradicate Protestant influences in Italy. Under Pope Paul IV, this inquisition was a reign of terror, killing many "heretics" on mere suspicion. Its victims included scientist-philosopher Giordano Bruno, who espoused Copernicus's theory that planets orbit the sun. He was burned at the stake in 1600 in Rome.

The Inquisition blighted many lands for centuries. In Portugal, records recount that 184 were burned alive and auto-da-fé processions contained as many as 1,500 "penitents" at a time. The Inquisition was brought by Spaniards to the American colonies, to punish Indians who reverted to native religions. A total of 879 heresy trials were recorded in Mexico in the late 1500s.

The horror persisted until modern times. The Spanish Inquisition was suppressed by

Ceremonious burning of convicted heretics at a religious "auto-da-fé" (act of faith) climaxed the Inquisition process. (Engraved in 1723 by Bernhard Picart. Library of Congress print collection.)

Joseph Bonaparte in 1808, restored by
Ferdinand VII in 1814, suppressed again in
1820, restored again in 1823, and finally
eradicated in 1834.

Lord Acton, himself a Catholic, wrote in
the late 1800s: "The principle of the Inquisition
was murderous. . . . The popes were not only
murderers in the great style, but they also
made murder a legal basis of the Christian
Church and a condition of salvation."

THE BLACK DEATH

Religious hate easily turns into ethnic hate.
Anti-Semitism that originated in a clash of
creeds soon took on a life of its own. Jews had
been spurned as religious pariahs, and they
subsequently were blamed for Christian
troubles not directly linked to religion.

When the bubonic plague stalked Europe in
1348, destroying nearly half the population,
hysterical Christians concluded that it was
caused by Jews poisoning wells. Massacres
ensued in about 300 cities. Mobs raged through
defenseless neighborhoods, murdering virtually
all residents—except a few allowed to save
themselves by accepting baptism.

At Speyer, Germany, Jewish bodies were
piled into huge wine casks and sent floating
down the Rhine. At Strasbourg, 2,000 Jews

were herded like cattle into a large wooden barn, which was set afire. On a single day, August 24, 1349, an estimated 6,000 Jews were slaughtered by inflamed Christians at Mainz. In several northern German cities, Jews were walled up in their homes to suffocate or starve.

At Benfeld, some Jews were burned and others were drowned in a swamp. In Bavaria, Christian mobs with pitchforks and sickles slashed through eighty Jewish communities, killing a reported 10,000. At Basel, Switzerland, Christian leaders burned 600 Jews at the stake as well-poisoners, and 140 of their children were forcibly baptized and taken away to be raised as Christians. Thus the Jewish community of Basel was entirely erased.

The Flagellants were a roaming army of penitents who whipped themselves bloody to expiate their sins in hope of inducing God to lift the plague. When the Flagellants arrived in Frankfurt in July, 1349, they stormed the Jewish quarter in a gory massacre. At Brussels, the approach of a Flagellant march sent local Christians on a rampage that killed 600 Jews.

In some locales, emperors and dukes attempted to protect Jews from the mobs. In other places, nobles joined the horror. The prince of Thuringia announced that he had

burned his Jews "for the honor of God" and
urged.colleagues to do likewise.

Historian Philip Ziegler counted 350
separate massacres of Jews by Christians
during three years of the Black Death. He
observed sadly: "It is a curious and somewhat
humiliating reflection on human nature that
the European, overwhelmed by what was
probably the greatest natural calamity ever to
strike his continent, reacted by seeking to rival
the cruelty of nature in the hideousness of his
own man-made atrocities."

WITCH-HUNTS

During the 1400s, the Holy Inquisition shifted its focus toward witchcraft, and the next three centuries witnessed a bizarre orgy of religious delusion. Agents of the church tortured untold thousands of women, and some men, into confessing that they flew through the sky on demonic missions, engaged in sex with Satan, turned themselves into animals, made themselves invisible, and performed other supernatural evils. Virtually all the accused were put to death. The number of victims is estimated widely from 100,000 to 2 million.

Pope Gregory IX originally authorized the killing of witches in the 1200s, and random witch trials were held, but the craze didn't catch fire until the 15th century. In 1484 Pope Innocent VIII issued a bull declaring the absolute reality of witches—thus it became heresy to doubt their existence. Prosecutions soared. The inquisitor Cumanus burned forty-one women the following year, and a colleague in the Piedmont of Italy executed 100.

Soon afterward, two Dominican inquisitors, Jakob Sprenger and Heinrich Kramer, published their infamous *Malleus Maleficarum* (Witches' Hammer) outlining a lurid litany of magical acts performed by witches and their imps, familiars, phantoms, demons, succubi, and incubi. It described how the evil women blighted crops, devoured children, caused disease, and wrought spells. The book was filled with witches' sexual acts and portrayed women as treacherous and contemptible. "All witchcraft comes from carnal lust, which is in women insatiable," they wrote. Modern psychology easily perceives the sexual neurosis of these priests—yet for centuries their book was the official manual used by inquisitors sending women to horrible deaths.

Witch-hunts flared in France, Germany, Hungary, Spain, Italy, Switzerland, Sweden, and nearly every corner of Europe—finally reaching England, Scotland, and the Massachusetts Bay Colony. Most of the victims were old women whose eccentricities roused

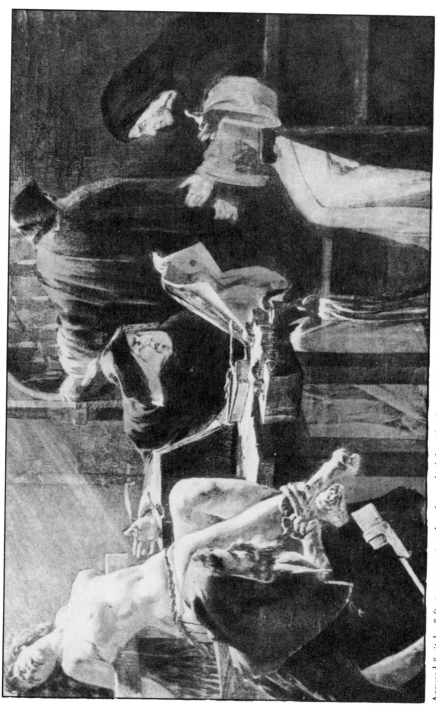

Accused "witches" first were stripped and searched for "devil's marks"—then the torture began. The process usually ended in execution. (By Jose Brito. Library of Congress print collection.)

suspicions of neighbors. Others were young, pretty women. Some were men. Many in continental Europe were simply citizens whose names were shrieked out by torture victims when commanded to identify fellow witches. (Torture wasn't used in England, so fewer perished there.)

The standard Inquisition procedure of isolating and grilling suspects was followed— plus an added step: the victims were stripped naked, shaved of all body hair, and "pricked." The *Malleus Maleficarum* specified that every witch bore a numb "devil's mark," which could be detected by jabbing with a sharp object. Inquisitors also looked for "witches' tits," blemishes that might be secret nipples whereby the women suckled their demons.

If the body search failed, the torture began. Fingernails were pulled out. Red-hot tongs were applied to breasts. "The women's sex organs provided special attraction for the male torturer," researcher Nancy van Vuuren wrote. Bodies were stretched on racks and wheels. "Arms came out of sockets and trysts with the Devil came out of the unlikeliest mouths," novelist Erica Jong wrote. Virtually every mangled and broken victim confessed—and was executed on the basis of the confession.

Burning at the stake was the chief fate of accused witches, but others were hanged, drowned, or crushed. (Library of Congress print collection.)

In the Basque region of Spain, church records dutifully report that Maria of Ituren admitted under torture that she and sister witches turned themselves into horses and galloped through the sky. In a district of France, 600 women confessed to copulating with demons.

The complete death toll is impossible to learn. Some historical records exist; others are gone. Various accounts say 5,000 witches were killed in the province of Alsace, 900 in the city of Bamberg, about 2,000 in Bavaria, 311 in Vaud, 167 at Grenoble, 157 at Wurzburg, 133 in a single day in Saxony. Some entire villages were exterminated.

The mania continued until the 18th century. In Scotland, an old woman was burned in 1722 after being convicted of turning her daughter into a pony and riding her to a witches' coven. In Germany, a nun was burned alive in the marketplace of Wurzburg in 1749 after other nuns testified that she climbed over convent walls in the form of a pig. The last legal execution of a witch occurred in Switzerland in 1782. By that time, various scientists and scholars had raised enough doubt about the reality of witchcraft to bring an end to the madness.

A profound irony of the witch-hunts is that they were directed, not by superstitious savages, but by learned bishops, judges, professors, and other leaders of society. The centuries of witch obsession demonstrated the terrible power of supernatural beliefs.

THE REFORMATION

Corruption in the medieval Catholic hierarchy was infamous. Pope John XII openly had love affairs, gave church treasure to a mistress, castrated one opponent, blinded another, and donned armor to lead an army. Benedict IX sold the papacy to a successor for 1,500 pounds of gold. Urban VI tortured and murdered his cardinals. Innocent VIII proudly acknowledged his illegitimate children and loaded them with church riches. Pope Boniface VII, whose name is omitted from official church listings, murdered two rival popes in the 10th century. Sergius III likewise killed two rivals for the papal throne. Benedict V dishonored a young girl and fled with the Vatican treasury. Clement VI sported with mistresses on ermine bed-linens. Boniface VIII sent troops to kill every resident of Palestrina and raze the city. Clement VII, while a papal legate, similarly ordered the slaughter of Cesena's 8,000 people, including the children. A previous Pope John XXIII (not the reformer of the 1950s) was desposed by a council in 1414—and Edward Gibbon drily recorded in *The Decline and Fall of the Roman Empire:* "The most serious charges were suppressed; the Vicar of Christ was accused only of piracy, murder, rape, sodomy, and incest." Alexander VI bought the papacy by bribing cardinals to elect him—then hosted sex orgies attended by his illegitimate children, Cesare and Lucrezia Borgia.

Regarding Alexander, scholar Barbara Tuchman recounted in *The March of Folly:*

"The pope presided over a banquet given by Cesare in the Vatican, famous in the annals of pornography as the Ballet of the Chestnuts. Soberly recorded by Burchard, 50 courtesans danced after dinner with the guests, 'at first clothed, then naked.' Chestnuts were then scattered among candelabra placed on the floor, 'which the courtesans, crawling on hands and knees among the candelabra, picked up, while the Pope, Cesare, and his sister Lucrezia looked on.' Coupling of guests and courtesans followed, with prizes in the form of fine silken

Reformer John Hus was burned as a heretic—then his ashes were carted to the Rhine River so his followers wouldn't preserve them as relics. (15th century woodcut. Library of Congress print collection.)

tunics and cloaks offered 'for those who could perform the act most often with the courtesans.' "

Cardinals, archbishops, abbots, bishops, priests, and monks kept concubines, pocketed church wealth, waged armed vendettas, and grew rich through simony, the selling of church offices and acts. Pope Innocent III ranted against his clergy: "All of them, from the highest to the lowest, do as it is said in the prophets: They are enthralled to avarice, love presents, and seek rewards; for the sake of bribes they pronounce the godless righteous. . . ."

The orgy of greed provoked protests. In the 1100s, priest Arnold of Brescia called for reform. He was defrocked, exiled, and excommunicated, but he persisted, rousing the people of Rome. Finally he was captured in 1155, hanged, and burned.

In England in the 1300s, professor-priest John Wycliffe denounced church corruption, rejected the doctrine of transubstantiation, and violated church law by translating the Bible into English for common people to read. After his death, his followers, called Lollards, were declared heretics. Many were captured, locked in stocks, and forced to renounce their beliefs.

Catholic troops under Gen. Tilly massacred the Protestants at Magdeburg in 1631. (From *Martyrs Mirror*, 1685, courtesy of Lancaster Mennonite Historical Society.)

Several were burned at the stake.

In Prague, priest John Hus embraced Wycliffe's teachings and denounced immorality among the clergy. He drew ardent followers. In 1412, three of these Hussites were executed for protesting the church's sale of indulgences (releases from punishment in Purgatory). Hus was excommunicated and exiled, but he continued. In 1415 he went to the Council of Constance, which had been convened to eradicate church corruption. Although he bore a letter of safe passage from the emperor, he was thrown in a dungeon, then burned. Hus's execution enraged his followers in Czechoslovakia, who formed an alliance for religious independence. Pope Martin V repeatedly sent crusades against them, but his armies were beaten. Finally, the church offered a compromise on a disputed point of theology—which caused Hussite factions to split, and one group joined the Catholic army in destroying the other.

In Florence, priest Girolamo Savonarola took up the cry for church reform. His fiery attacks caused opponents to obtain his excommunication. He continued preaching until he was jailed, condemned by a papal commission, and hanged and burned with two of his followers in 1498.

A priest blesses hanging victims in this famous etching from the Thirty Years War. (By Jacques Callot, 1592–1635. Metropolitan Museum of Art.)

After these abortive rebellions, the *real* rebellion exploded in 1517. Martin Luther nailed his 95 theses to the Wittenberg Church door, triggering the Reformation, which plunged Christendom into a century of Catholic-Protestant slaughter.

Soon after Luther's fateful revolt, one of his most fanatical adherents in Germany carried the rebellion to a bizarre extreme. Priest Thomas Muntzer preached that the godless must be annihilated. He roused 8,000 peasants into a ragtag army and led the Peasants' War of 1525. His hymn-singing amateur soldiers were wiped out by trained legions, and Muntzer was tortured and executed.

In Switzerland, a separate revolt was led by Ulrich Zwingli. Swiss cities adopted Zwingli's modified Christianity, while rural cantons (districts) remained Catholic. City Protestants and country Catholics clashed in two local wars. In the second, in 1531, Zwingli was killed.

In Germany, Lutheran princes met at Schmalkald and formed a defensive alliance against Catholic power. Holy Roman Emperor Charles V sent Catholic armies to annihilate the Protestants. He achieved some victories, but in 1555 he was forced to accept the Peace of Augsburg, which allowed 300 German local

The Counterreformation brought armed assaults on some Protestant towns—such as this attack at Tirano, northern Italy, in 1606. (From *Martyrs Mirror*, 1685, courtesy of Lancaster Mennonite Historical Society.)

rulers to decide whether their districts would be Catholic or Protestant.

The Peace of Augsburg recognized the right of Protestant "heretics" to exist in Germany—but other Catholic countries granted no such tolerance. In Spain, the Inquisition began exterminating suspected Protestants. Multitudes were strangled and burned at a great auto-da-fé in 1559 held in honor of King Philip II, son of Emperor Charles V. Archbishop Bartolome de Carranza of Toledo was imprisoned 17 years because he favored the tolerant views of Dutch Catholic thinker Desiderius Erasmus. In Italy, the Inquisition was revived in 1542 to hunt those with Protestant leanings.

In Switzerland, after the death of Zwingli, John Calvin became the driving force of Protestantism. He created a rigid theocracy in Geneva. Morality police inspected household behavior. Harsh punishments were administered for ribaldry, dancing, card-playing, drinking, and other amusements. Theological nonconformists were put to death. Michael Servetus was burned for doubting the Trinity. Jacques Gruet was beheaded for blasphemy. Calvin urged the burning of witches.

A young Huguenot nobleman who killed the Catholic Duc de Guise was drawn and quartered in 1563. (German engraving. Library of Congress print collection.)

Throughout Europe, the number of wars, expulsions, massacres, and executions that accompanied the Reformation are almost beyond counting. Following are the major Christian-versus-Christian bloodbaths:

France

Protestantism sprouted in Catholic France, and King Henry II vowed to destroy it. He created a heresy court that became known as the Burning Chamber because of its standard sentence for Huguenots (the French name for Protestants). In 1559, France and Spain signed a treaty agreeing to extirpate Protestantism from their lands.

For a while, French queen mother Catherine de Medici allowed Huguenots to worship in certain locales. But Catholic dukes massacred the worshipers—setting off religious warfare that broke out again and again. Altogether, eight Huguenot wars occurred between 1562 and 1589. Each side was brutal. Huguenot soldiers smashed church ornaments and hunted priests like animals. One captain wore a necklace of priests' ears. A French observer reported:

Catholics killing Protestants in the St. Bartholomew's Day massacre, Paris, Aug. 24, 1572. (Painting by Francois Dubois, 16th century. Musee Cantonal des Beaux Arts, Lausanne, France.)

"It would be impossible to tell you what barbarous cruelties are committed by both sides. Where the Huguenot is master, he ruins the images and demolishes the sepulchres and tombs. On the other hand, the Catholic kills, murders, and drowns all those whom he knows to be of that sect, until the rivers overflow with them."

Pope Pius sent troops to France to help fight the Huguenots, and ordered the commander to kill every prisoner taken. Pius was later canonized as a saint.

After the third war, Catherine de Medici sought to end the horror by arranging the marriage of her daughter to a young Huguenot prince, Henry of Navarre. Perversely, when Huguenots gathered in Paris for the wedding under a promise of safe passage, Catherine plotted with Catholic dukes to assassinate the Huguenot military leader, Admiral Gaspard de Coligny. The assassin missed, merely wounding the admiral—so Catherine and the dukes hastily decided to murder all Huguenots before they had time to counterattack. On the night of August 24, 1572—St. Bartholomew's Day— Catholic troops swept through Huguenot neighborhoods in Paris, slaughtering thousands. Coligny was beheaded. Other massacres were staged throughout France.

Huguenots hanging, stabbing, and chopping Catholic monks. (From the print collection of the Pierpont Morgan Library, New York.)

Coligny's head was sent to Rome, where Pius's successor, Pope Gregory XIII, received it joyfully. He and the whole college of cardinals offered a mass of thanksgiving. The pope struck a medal celebrating the Catholic victory and commissioned the artist Giorgio Vasari to paint a fresco of the triumph over the Huguenots.

The St. Bartholomew's Day massacre naturally triggered a fourth Huguenot war, and four more followed. Finally, Huguenot Henry of Navarre was offered the crown as king of France if he would convert to Catholicism. He did so, saying cynically, "Paris is worth a mass." He issued the Edict of Nantes allowing Protestants to worship. After his death, however, all civil rights were stripped from Huguenots and they were persecuted ruthlessly. More civil wars erupted in the 1620s. In 1715, King Louis XIV proudly declared that all Protestantism had been suppressed in France.

Hundreds of thousands of Huguenots fled during the horrors. One colony settled in Florida, preceding what is now St. Augustine. A Spanish expedition discovered the colony in 1565 and killed virtually every person. The Spanish commander erected a sign saying the settlers were executed "not as Frenchmen but as Lutherans."

Protestants of Haarlem, Holland, were executed in 1573 by Catholic troops in the Duke of Alva's holy war. (From the New York Public Library print collection.)

The Low Countries

When Protestantism took root in the Low
Countries, Catholic rulers vowed to obliterate
it at any cost. Dowager queen Mary of
Hungary, regent of Flanders, ordered execution
of all heretics, "care being taken only that the
provinces are not entirely depopulated." The
Inquisition killed multitudes. Mary decreed that
Protestants who recanted would be spared
burning; instead, the men would be killed by
sword and the women buried alive.

The great Flemish mapmaker Gerardus
Mercator was caught in a roundup of suspected
Lutherans in 1544. Of those arrested with him,
two were burned, two were buried alive, and
one was beheaded. Mercator finally was
released through efforts of his parish priest.

Spanish King Philip II, ruler of Holland and
Belgium, was obsessed with halting
Protestantism in those lands. He revived the
Inquisition and commanded: "Let all prisoners
be put to death, and suffer them no longer to
escape through the neglect, weakness, and bad
faith of the judges." Protestants rebelled and
burned 400 Catholic churches. The Duke of
Alva was sent to smash Protestant towns. His
onslaught was called "the Spanish fury." He

Catholic troops under the Duke of Alva tortured and burned Protestants in Holland in the 1560s. (From *Martyrs Mirror*, 1685, courtesy of Lancaster Mennonite Historical Society.)

killed thousands in Antwerp and massacred Haarlem Protestants in 1573. He set up a heresy court, popularly called the Bloody Tribunal, which sent throngs of suspected Protestants to be executed. A Dutch chronicler wrote:

"The gallows, the wheel, stakes, trees along the highways, were laden with carcasses or limbs of those who had been hanged, beheaded, or roasted."

One of the victims was Count Egmont, whose martyrdom was commemorated by Beethoven in the Egmont Overture.

In the northern districts of Holland, Protestants led by William of Orange declared their independence from Catholic Spain. Philip II offered 25,000 crowns of gold for William's assassination, and he was killed in 1584. But William's militant Calvinists continued fighting until they secured Protestant independence for the northern provinces.

England

The Catholic Church decreed that the Bible could be printed only in Latin, restricting it to priests and scholars. Printing it in a common language for common people was punishable by death. In England in the 1520s, William Tyndale sought permission to translate the New Testament into English so "every plowboy" might read it. The request put his life in danger, and he fled to Lutheran territory in Germany. He completed a translation and smuggled copies back to England—where they were seized and burned by Catholic bishops. Tyndale eventually was captured in Antwerp by Catholic authorities, who tried him for heresy and had him strangled and burned. (Later, much of Tyndale's magnificent prose was incorporated into the King James version of the Bible.)

English King Henry VIII, who cynically used religion for power, had attempted to capture and try Tyndale. Henry also denounced Martin Luther and Protestantism, for which the pope gratefully proclaimed him a "Defender of the Faith."

But when Henry wanted to divorce Catherine of Aragon, and the pope refused permission, the headstrong king arranged to divorce England from Catholicism. Parliament made the king, not the pope, supreme head of the church in England. Henry chose an obedient archbishop, Thomas Cranmer, who dissolved his unwanted marriage. Henry also seized the rich lands of formerly Catholic monasteries throughout England. The pope excommunicated Henry and tried to mount a crusade against England, but Catholic rulers around Europe declined to participate.

Henry fashioned a formal Church of England retaining most Catholic dogmas—and made it a capital offense to doubt those dogmas. Thus he executed stubborn Catholics such as Sir Thomas More, who voiced loyalty to the pope, and he also burned Lutherans who questioned transubstantiation. After Henry was succeeded by his 10-year-old son, Edward VI, further breaks from Catholicism were achieved by Archbishop Cranmer.

Edward was succeeded in 1553 by Mary I, daughter of Henry and Catherine of Aragon—and she became history's "Bloody Mary." An ardent Catholic, she sought to restore England to Catholicism through terror. In three years, she burned 300 Protestants alive. Archbishop Cranmer wavered, first embracing Catholicism, then renouncing it. He was sent to the stake—but he impressed the crowd by declaring his shame at recanting, and thrust into the flames his hand that had betrayed him by signing an oath to the pope.

When bishops Nicholas Ridley and Hugh Latimer went to the stake, the latter declared: "Be of good comfort, Master Ridley, and play the man. We shall this day light such a candle by God's grace in England as I trust shall never be put out." He was right. The English, sickened by the executions and impressed by the martyrs' bravery, turned intensely Protestant.

When Elizabeth I succeeded to the throne, she sought to end the religious killings. But she was caught in a church crossfire. From one side, Catholics plotted against her life and staged a rebellion in the north. From the other side, extreme Protestant Puritans and Separatists raged against popery and "Romish dregs" in the Church of England. In retaliation, Parliament passed harsh laws making it treason to celebrate the Catholic mass, and also forbidding Puritan worship. A fine of twenty pounds a month was imposed on anyone not attending Anglican services.

About 200 Catholics were executed as traitors under Elizabeth—and Mary, Queen of Scots, was beheaded because Catholics conspired to put her on Elizabeth's throne. In addition, three fanatical Puritans were put to death.

Amid this strife, King Philip II sent the Spanish Armada on a holy mission to force England's return to Catholicism. But that too failed, and England remained Protestant.

Scotland

Before Mary, Queen of Scots, met the headsman in England, she participated in Catholic-Protestant bloodshed in Scotland.

The Reformation brought the same horror to Scotland as to other lands. The Catholic parliament banned Lutheran books and preaching. Cardinal David Beaton burned Protestant leaders Patrick Hamilton and George Wishart. Then their followers murdered Beaton, hung his body from the wall of St. Andrew's Castle, and barricaded themselves in the castle.

John Knox became chief of the besieged Protestants. When French Catholic troops finally helped Scottish Catholics seize the castle, Knox and his colleagues were sent into slavery aboard French galleys. English intervention obtained his release nineteen months later, and he began preaching in England and on the continent.

Scotland was ruled by Mary of Lorraine, of France's fiercely Catholic House of Guise. She denounced Scot Protestants as heretics. Protestant lairds rebelled, summoned Knox from Geneva to be their voice, and waged war against Catholic strongholds. They seized Edinburgh and, with English help, gained control of Scotland. A Protestant parliament renounced the pope and decreed death to anyone who attended Catholic mass more than twice.

Mary of Lorraine died and her 18-year-old daughter, also Mary, came from France to be queen of Scots. She was an immature Catholic ruler in a land seething with Protestantism. She might have coped, but she married a Catholic scoundrel, then conspired to have him murdered, then married his chief assassin. Protestant lairds rebelled again. They defeated Mary's Catholic troops at Carberry Hill near Edinburgh and jailed her in an island castle.

Mary escaped, and another Catholic army rallied around her—but it too was smashed by Protestant forces. Mary fled to England, where she was imprisoned eighteen years by Queen Elizabeth, until Catholic insurrection plots finally led to her beheading.

Thirty Years' War

The last great spasm of the Reformation was
its worst. The Thirty Years' War, from 1618 to
1648, killed millions in Central Europe and left
Germany a wasteland of misery.

It began because Catholic Habsburg rulers
of the Holy Roman Empire tried to suppress
growing Calvinism in regions already
smoldering with Catholic-Lutheran tensions.
Evangelical princes formed a defensive alliance,
the Protestant Union. The other side formed
the Catholic League. They faced each other like
ticking bombs—which finally exploded over a
trifle: Protestant nobles entered the imperial
palace in Prague and threw two Catholic
ministers out a window into a dungheap,
touching off war.

Catholic armies quickly slaughtered the
Protestant forces. The conflict might have
ended then, but Catholic Emperor Ferdinand II
decided to eradicate Protestantism entirely. The
faith was outlawed and cruel persecution was
inflicted.

Protestants appealed for foreign help, and
Protestant King Christian IV of Denmark sent
an army to their rescue. Lutheran and Calvinist
German princes joined him. Once again the

Protestants were defeated, once again
Ferdinand resumed religious oppression, and
once again the victims sought outside aid.

Next, Protestant King Gustav Adolph of
Sweden marched into Germany to rescue his
fellow believers. His soldiers sang Martin
Luther's hymn *Ein 'Feste Burg* in battle. Terrible
slaughter occurred. A Catholic army captured
Magdeburg and massacred its Protestant
residents. King Gustav was killed, and his
troops wreaked vengeance on Catholic peasants.

Eventually the war turned more political
than religious. Catholic France entered on the
side of the Protestants, in an attempt to cripple
the rival Habsburgs. The killing dragged on
decade after decade until both sides were too
exhausted to continue.

The Thirty Year's War was a human
catastrophe. It settled nothing, and it killed
uncountable multitudes. One estimate says
Germany's population dropped from 18 million
to 4 million. Hunger and deprivation followed.
Too few people remained to plant fields, rebuild
cities, or conduct education or commerce.

This disaster helped break the historic
entwinement of Christianity and politics. The
concluding Peace of Westphalia prescribed an
end to the pope's control over civil governments.

ANABAPTISTS

Although Catholics and Protestants were mortal enemies during most of the Reformation, they united to kill certain Christians for the crime of double baptism.

"A larger proportion of Anabaptists were martyred for their faith than any other Christian group in history—including even the early Christians on whom they modeled themselves," British scholar Bamber Gascoigne wrote.

The Anabaptists rejected traditional infant baptism. They said baptism should be for thinking adults, so they rebaptized mature converts. When they first did so in Zwingli's Switzerland in 1525, Protestant leaders of Zurich sentenced them to death, basing the verdict on the Justinian Code, which mandates

This Anabaptist was executed in 1592 at Weir by drowning—deemed a fitting end for believers in double baptism. (From *Martyrs Mirror*, 1685, courtesy of Lancaster Mennonite Historical Society.)

execution for baptizing twice. The Swiss Anabaptists were ordered drowned—which was deemed a fitting end for those wanting immersion.

Despite the persecution, Anabaptism spread rapidly to the Low Countries and Germany. At the Diet of Speyer in 1529, both Catholics and Lutherans agreed to put Anabaptists to death. Martin Luther publicly affirmed the edict in 1531. Around Europe, many were drowned, burned, beheaded.

During the slaughter, one group of Anabaptists turned to bizarre behavior. They seized control of Munster, Germany, and banished all Catholics and Protestants who wouldn't convert to the new faith. Outside the city walls, the bishop of Munster brought an army and began a siege. Inside the walls, Anabaptist leader John of Leyden proclaimed himself king of the New Zion, took several wives, and imposed the death penalty for numerous infractions. Historian Hendrick van Loon recounted:

"In that community of starving men and suffering children came the period of hallucinations when the populace suffered from a diversity of religious manias; when the marketplace was crowded day and night with

This Anabaptist teacher was beaten in a torture chamber before she was burned at Maastricht in 1570. (From *Martyrs Mirror*, 1685, courtesy of Lancaster Mennonite Historical Society.)

Clergymen burying an Anabaptist woman alive at Brussels in 1597. (From *Martyrs Mirror*, 1685, courtesy of Lancaster Mennonite Historical Society.)

While cross-bearing priests look on, the executioner finishes off an Anabaptist couple burned at Ghent in 1554. (From *Martyrs Mirror*, 1685, courtesy of Lancaster Mennonite Historical Society.)

thousands of men and women awaiting the trumpet blasts of the angel Gabriel. Then came the period of terror, when the prophet kept up the courage of his flock by a constant orgy of blood and cut the throat of one of his own queens."

Finally the bishop's army captured Munster and wrought vengeance. The Anabaptist leaders were tortured to death with red-hot pincers and their bodies were hung in iron cages from a church steeple, where they remained for many years.

"Such leaders as had escaped the carnage at Munster were hunted down like rabbits and killed wherever found," Van Loon added.

Surviving fragments of the Anabaptist movement eventually became the modern Mennonites, Amish, and Hutterians.

PURITANS

England had the double misfortune to suffer two religious splits. The first, when the Church of England was severed from Rome, produced a famous parade of executions. The second, when Puritans broke with the Church of England, was more lethal.

Although Puritanism had been officially outlawed under Queen Elizabeth I, it continued to grow, turning increasingly rigid in its attempt to "purify" the Anglican Church by purging hints of Catholicism. Historian J. R. Green wrote:

"The absolute devotion of the Puritan to a Supreme Will tended more and more to rob him of all sense of measure and proportion in common matters. Little things became great things in the glare of religious zeal, and the godly man learned to shrink from a surplice, or a mince pie at Christmas, as he shrank from impurity or a lie. Life became hard, rigid, colorless, as it became intense."

Puritans renounced frivolity. Lord Macaulay noted that Puritans "hated bear-baiting, not because it gave pain to the bear, but because it gave pleasure to the spectators."

When Puritans called upon King James I to reform the church, he furiously bade them conform to Anglicanism. "I will make them conform or I will harry them out of the land, or else worse—hang them." His harsh measures caused some Puritans to begin moving to Holland and New England.

James was succeeded by his son, Charles I, whose ruthless archbishop of Canterbury, William Laud, persecuted Puritans. He tried them in the secretive Star Chamber and had them scourged, pilloried, or imprisoned—and sometimes had their ears cropped, their foreheads branded, or their noses split.

Laud sought to impose an Anglican prayer book on Scottish congregations. They rebelled in the Bishops Wars in 1639. Charles summoned parliament to raise money for an army to fight in Scotland. But this "Short

Cromwell's Puritan "Ironsides" troops in a frenzied attack on an Anglican regiment. (Library of Congress print collection.)

Parliament" hesitated, and the king dissolved it. Then he summoned another, the "Long Parliament"—which was his undoing.

The Parliament contained a majority of Puritans, and they began dismembering Charles's government. Archbishop Laud was jailed and later executed. The Star Chamber was abolished. A petition was passed giving Parliament control over the Anglican Church. Charles made an abortive attempt to arrest the top Puritan legislators. This spurred them to form a rival government and raise troops. The king fled and rallied his regiments. Civil war was on.

Parliament member Oliver Cromwell rose to leadership of the Puritan army (which also contained Presbyterians and dissidents of other sects). Cromwell knew that religious fervor could produce the fighting spirit that won battles. His soldiers, called "Ironsides," carried Bibles and sang hymns. He delayed battles to lead prayer or chant psalms—then sent his troops to kill with holy zeal. All his victories were attributed to the Lord. After slaughtering an Anglican force, Cromwell said that "God made them as stubble to our swords."

The victorious Cromwell obtained the execution of King Charles. Then he took his soldiers to Ireland to kill rebellious Catholics. The English forces were a death machine. Irish historian Seumas MacManus recounted:

"[A]ll 17,000 of the flower of the Puritan army . . . were extraordinary men, his Ironsides—Bible-reading, psalm-singing soldiers of God—fearfully daring, fiercely fanatical, papist hating, looking on this land as being assigned to them, the chosen people, by their God. And looking on the inhabitants as idol-worshiping Canaanites who were cursed of God, and to be extirpated by the sword. They came with minds inflamed. . . ."

First these holy warriors captured Drogheda, and Cromwell ordered the execution of surrendered Catholics and their priests, calling it "a righteous judgment of God upon these barbarous wretches." Then the same treatment was inflicted upon town after town until the Catholic resistance was destroyed. Women and priests were massacred. British writer Thomas Carlyle later rhapsodized: "Oliver Cromwell came as a soldier of God the Just, terrible as Death, relentless as Doom, doing God's judgments on the enemies of God."

Cromwell returned to England and made himself a holy dictator, the Lord Protector. But his death in 1658 was followed by an Anglican backlash called the Restoration. Cromwell's body was unearthed and hanged, and his head mounted on a pole above Westminster Hall. Anglican uniformity laws were passed, forcing 1,800 Puritan rectors out of their posts. Puritan, Presbyterian, and other dissident worship was outlawed. Baptist minister John Bunyan was imprisoned twelve years, during which he wrote *Pilgrim's Progress.* Troops were sent to find non-Anglicans worshiping in fields.

Eventually, the death penalty was imposed for attending a non-Anglican service. Women and children were tortured to make them reveal the whereabouts of men running from arrest. An 18-year-old girl was drowned in Solway Inlet for refusing to renounce Presbyterianism. Small religious uprisings occurred in 1666 and 1679. During the reign of King James II in the 1680s, the hunt for hard-line Presbyterians called Cameronians was known as "the killing time."

Meanwhile, Puritans who went to Massachusetts to escape religious persecution became notorious for persecuting others. They created a religious police state where doctrinal deviation could lead to flogging, pillorying, banishment, hanging—-or cutting off ears, or

In Puritan Massachusetts, religious nonconformists suffered this fate—and much worse. (An 1892 lithograph from the Library of Congress print collection.)

boring through the tongue with a hot iron. Preaching Quaker beliefs was a capital offense. Four stubborn Quakers defied this law and were hanged. In the 1690s, fear of witches seized the colony. Twenty alleged witches were killed and 150 others imprisoned.

ORTHODOX WAR

Five horrible centuries of religious persecution—from the 1100s through the 1500s—decimated the Jewish population of Western Europe. Vast numbers were killed. (Historian Dagobert Runes estimated that 3.5 million Jews died at the hands of Christians during the long epoch of religious persecution.) Multitudes of other Jews saved themselves by turning Christian. Many Jewish children were forcibly baptized and taken away. Country after country expelled Jews, seizing their possessions and sending them penniless into exile. Those not expelled were quarantined to ghettos and forced to wear humiliating identifying badges.

Desperately seeking a place of safety, Jews flooded into Poland, then a primitive region.

There, they were able to settle and regain their vitality. Nobles enlisted them as farm "rendars" (administrators) overseeing serfs. After Poland annexed the Ukraine in 1569, Jews were sent in to colonize the territory. The Jewish population of Poland rose to 500,000, the largest in the world.

While the Jews were thriving, the Ukrainian Cossacks—of Eastern Orthodox religion—were turning mutinous against their Catholic rulers and Jewish overseers. A holy war-style rebellion was brewing, and it was triggered in 1648 when Ukrainian officer Bogdan Chmielnicki (or Bohdan Kmelnitsky) preached hatred of Jews and Catholic Poles. Orthodox peasants and priests rallied behind him in a gory uprising.

The onslaught rapidly overran the furthermost Jewish settlements and sent survivors fleeing back toward Poland. The Orthodox horde pursued. Major massacres occurred at Nemirov, Tulchin, Bar, Narol, and other cities. As had happened frequently during the past five centuries, many captured Jews were given a choice of conversion or death.

Chmielnicki has been called a Cossack Cromwell because of the religious nature of his warfare. Upon suffering setbacks, he sought help from the Russians, who also invaded Poland and continued the killing of Jews. Altogether, an estimated 100,000 died in 300 communities.

At the end, the Ukraine was wrested away from Catholic Poland and annexed to the Orthodox Russian empire.

ENLIGHTENMENT

During the 1700s, religion's throttlehold upon Europe slowly loosened. Religious killing still occurred, but with decreasing frequency. Sporadic examples:

In 1723, the bishop of Gdansk, Poland, demanded the expulsion of Jews. The city council declined, but the bishop's exhortations roused a mob that invaded the ghetto and beat the residents to death.

Women still were burned occasionally as witches—in Scotland in 1722, in Germany in 1749, in Switzerland in 1782.

From 1702 to 1710, Louis XIV's efforts to stamp out Protestantism caused Camisards of southern France to burn Catholic churches and kill priests. Catholic troops were sent in, slaughtering whole villages. Camisard leaders were executed.

The Inquisition was still alive, chiefly in Spain, but its horrors were few (perhaps because Spain had hardly any secret Jews, Muslims, or Protestants left to kill).

In 1715, Protestants were violently persecuted in the Rhineland Palatinate, and in 1732, Archbishop Firmian forcibly expelled 20,000 Protestants from Salzburg province.

Christians still accused Jews of stealing holy wafers and stabbing them to crucify Jesus again. An execution for host-nailing happened in Nancy, France, in 1761. Christians still accused Jews of sacrificing Gentile children, but massacres were rare. A late exception was the killing of 128 Jews at Bucharest in 1801 after Orthodox priests raised the blood libel.

Why did church atrocities recede in the West? Because a new social climate was spreading—the Age of Reason, the Enlightenment. Philosopher Hegel called it "the Age of Intelligence." The growth of scientific thinking and open discourse brought an awakening of human rights: a sense that people should be allowed to hold differing beliefs without risking death.

This freedom didn't come easily. Maverick thinkers paid for it by placing themselves in jeopardy. In the 1720s, English writer Thomas Woolston voiced doubt of the Resurrection and other Bible miracles, and he was put under house arrest for the remainder of his life. French intellectual Denis Diderot, editor of the first encyclopedia, was jailed briefly for writing irreligious thoughts. Many nonconformist thinkers had their writings seized and burned.

The supreme genius of the Enlightenment was Francois Marie Arouet, known forever as Voltaire. A celebrated playwright and wit, he changed late in life into a fearless crusader against religious cruelty and injustice. Disregarding his personal safety, he wrote vehement attacks on the church's record of brutality.

"Every sensible man, every honorable man, must hold the Christian sect in horror," he said. He told Frederick the Great that Christianity "is the most ridiculous, the most absurd, and bloody religion that has ever infected the world."

Voltaire's onslaughts put him in danger. His irreverent *Philosophical Dictionary* was publicly burned in Paris, Geneva, and Holland, and was banned by the Holy Office. Louis XV banished him from Paris. He lived in exile, finally buying an estate on the French-Swiss border, so he might escape into Switzerland if French Catholics came for him, and into France if sought by Swiss Calvinists. From this retreat, he corresponded with thinkers throughout Europe—and sympathizers everywhere began following his struggle for tolerance.

Voltaire protested French Catholic cruelties to Protestants, such as a 1752 edict nullifying all Protestant marriages and baptisms. More directly, Voltaire became a defender of Protestant victims of injustice, hiring lawyers and waging long court battles in their behalf. Some of his cases:

• Huguenot cotton trader Jean Calas was charged with murdering his son, allegedly because the youth was planning to convert to Catholicism. Actually, the son never had contemplated conversion, and had committed suicide in a fit of depression. Catholic judges found the family guilty in 1762 and had the father killed barbarically: all four of his limbs were broken in two places, then he was strangled and burned. The family property was seized and the other members were banished from France. Voltaire, incensed, wrote pamphlets against the outrage and enlisted influential friends to seek redress. Finally a new trial was ordered in 1765. Forty judges unanimously declared Calas innocent. The family property was restored and the king paid compensation to the widow.

• Two teen-age boys of Abbeville, Chevalier de La Barre and Gaillard d'Etallonde, were accused of wearing their hats while a church procession passed, and singing irreverent songs and mutilating a crucifix that stood on a bridge. D'Etallonde escaped before trial, but his companion was condemned to have his tongue cut out, his right hand cut off, and to be burned at the stake. Voltaire sought leniency. The case was appealed to parliament in Paris. The clergy demanded death, and parliament acceded, substituting the more merciful penalty of decapitation. The horrible sentence was carried out on July 1, 1766. Voltaire helped d'Etallonde enter the Prussian army and worked for his eventual rehabilitation in court.

• Jean Pierre Espinas spent twenty-three years as a convict oarsman in a penal galley ship—for the crime of giving lodging to a Protestant minister for one night. Voltaire obtained his release.

• Claude Chaumont likewise was sentenced to a galley bench for attending a Protestant worship service. Voltaire secured his freedom.

Voltaire's exposure of such cases gave them international notoriety. He also raised outcries against injustices not related to religion. Under his bombardment, France began to abandon torture and mutilation. Voltaire's efforts taught kindred spirits around the world how to fight for human rights.

Enlightenment ideas found fertile ground in the revolutionary new democracy taking shape in America. Thomas Jefferson, an intense scholar, knew the horrors of Old World abuses and devised safeguards against them. He insisted on "a wall of separation" to prevent the church from using the state, or vice versa. He was proud of his authorship of Virginia's statute of religious freedom and had it cited on his tombstone. It begins: "No man shall be compelled to frequent or support any religious worship, place or ministry whatever. . . ."

Thomas Paine, the fiery pamphleteer of the Revolution, waged war against church oppression in his later years in England and France. In *The Age of Reason*, he attacked Christianity as a system of superstition that "produces fanatics" and "serves the purposes of despotism." When the book reached England, several sellers were convicted of blasphemy and jailed.

Gradually, the Age of Enlightenment wrought profound change. People no longer believed in religion intensely enough to torture, burn, and massacre each other over points of theology. Thus religious killing came to an end in Western Europe.

But in some other parts of the world, it never stopped.

SEPOY MUTINY

The ominous power of religious taboos was demonstrated in India in 1857. Both Hindu and Muslim taboos combined to trigger the Sepoy Mutiny, which took thousands of lives.

Britain's commercial East India Company, ruling India as a lucrative colony, bought new Enfield rifles for its quarter-million mercenary native soldiers, called sepoys. The rifles used paper cartridges that had to be bitten open. Unfortunately, the cartridges were greased with animal tallow. This enraged both Hindu sepoys, to whom cows were sacred, and Muslim soldiers, to whom pigs were unclean.

The uprising began at Meerut. Eighty-five sepoys refused to use the cartridges. British officers clapped them in chains and sentenced each to ten years at hard labor. Soon afterward, the whole native garrison erupted in a killing frenzy. Sepoys stormed the stockade, released their chained comrades, and burned the military camp. Then they ravaged the city, killing every European they could find.

Many of the sepoys galloped to Delhi and slaughtered the city's Europeans. Then the rebellion spread through the Ganges valley. At Kanpur, besieged and starving British troops surrendered on a promise that they and their wives and children would be allowed to leave safely. They were escorted as far as the Ganges river, then massacred. Some female survivors were kept several days, then executed with knives. At Lucknow, the surrounded British garrison and a few loyal sepoys held out five months until rescue forces arrived.

Fortunately for the British, Sikhs of the Punjab region hated both Hindus and Muslims, so Sikh sepoys remained loyal and helped crush the mutineers. Upon winning, the Britons took revenge as barbaric as the original mutiny.

Of course the Sepoy Mutiny wasn't caused solely by tallow on cartridges. Many Indians had resented the Victorian empire-builders who controlled their country. British attempts to change the culture—banning suttee and infanticide, allowing widows to remarry, permitting converts from Hinduism to inherit property—were seen as religious intrusions. The arrival of British Christian missionaries compounded the unrest. The cartridge grease smoothed the slide into carnage.

After the tragedy, Britain's parliament abolished the civilian East India Company and put the Indian colony under government control.

BAHA'I

The youngest worldwide faith began a century
and a half ago—and it has suffered horribly at
the hands of Muslims ever since.

The Baha'is arose from a branch of Shi'ites
called "the Twelvers," who prayerfully await
the return of a long-vanished "Twelfth Imam."
In 1844, a holy from Iran man announced that
he was the Bab, the "gate" through whom the
Twelfth Imam spoke. He began drawing
followers, called Bab'is. They included a young
woman poet who wanted Muslim women freed
from subjugation.

The clergy and the Islamic government
sought to quell the fervent movement.
Violence grew. The Bab was imprisoned for
years, then shot by a firing squad in 1850. The
Bab'is became more mutinous, and the reprisals

more harsh. In 1852, two Bab'is tried to kill the shah, triggering a bloodbath. Islamic forces massacred an estimated 20,000 Bab'is, including the woman poet. Streets of Teheran were filled with blood.

Surviving Bab'i leaders and their families were sent into captivity in other Muslim lands—first to Baghdad, then Constantinople, then Adrianople. One leader, Baha'ullah, proclaimed himself the new divine emissary. His half-brother vied for the title, and the group split. Turks sent Baha'ullah and his followers, the Baha'is, to a prison at Acre. The half-brother's smaller group was sent to captivity on Cyprus.

From confinement, Baha'ullah renounced violence and wrote epistles to growing clusters of the faithful. He died in 1892 and his two sons disputed for leadership. One prevailed. The Young Turk rebellion of 1908 finally freed the Baha'i leaders after fifty-six years of incarceration.

Meanwhile, proliferating Baha'is in Iran suffered more than their jailed leaders. Shi'ite mullahs denounced them as heretics and sorcerers. Mobs sporadically attacked them. When a shah was assassinated by a Muslim terrorist in 1896, Baha'is were blamed and

Muslims killing a Bahá'í. (From the Arabic magazine *Imá'mat*, 1911, courtesy Bahá'í Office of Public Information, Wilmette, Ill.)

massacred. Waves of killing recurred in 1903, 1906, and during World War I. A young Baha'i woman who escaped to Canada wrote:

"In 1910 my mother's father and grandfather were first shot in the legs and then hanged because they were Baha'is. Her grandfather did not die immediately, so they put some sticks under his feet and burned him. When my parents were first married, their crops were confiscated and their house was burned."

Iran's Shi'ites constantly attempted to force Baha'is to convert to Islam. Hostility periodically burst out of control. In 1955 a fiery mullah, Sheik Muhammad Falsafi, preached over Iranian radio that faithful Muslims should rise up against the "false religion." Public rage soared. The shah's army seized the domed Baha'i temple in Teheran, and smiling colonels and mullahs were photographed smashing it. The minister of the interior proclaimed in parliament that Baha'ism was outlawed. Throughout Iran, a storm of murder, rape, beating, pillage, arson, and destruction ravaged the defenseless minority. The United Nations intervened, and passions finally subsided.

Persecution pervaded other Muslim lands. In 1962 in Morocco, some Baha'is were

Bahá'ís, including a father and son at left, were chained together by Muslim authorities in 1896. (Photo courtesy of Bahá'í Office of Public Information, Wilmette, Ill.)

sentenced to death for winning converts from Islam. International protests forced Morocco to relent. In 1987 in Egypt, 48 Baha'is were sentenced to prison for practicing their religion.

Another orgy of Baha'i-killing arose in Iran in the 1980s after the fundamentalist Shi'ite seizure of the country. The "heresy" was officially outlawed. A chief religious judge declared:

"The Iranian nation has determined to establish the government of God on Earth. Therefore, it cannot tolerate the perverted Baha'is, who are instruments of Satan and followers of the devil and of the superpowers. . . . Before it is too late, the Baha'is should recant Baha'ism."

Public hangings, jailings, torture, forced conversions, and mob lynchings were inflicted on many of Iran's 300,000 Baha'is. They were thrown out of their jobs, schools, and homes. Pensions of the elderly were cut off. About 200 who refused to convert to Islam were executed—including teen-agers and women. Even high-school girls were put to death. In some cases, after firing squads shot the "heretics," their families were forced to pay for the bullets before they could claim the bodies. About 40,000 Baha'is fled the nation.

In 1985 more than a hundred members of the U.S. Congress signed a resolution condemning Iran's "relentless acts of savagery against the innocent Baha'is." The State Department's human-rights chief called Iran's religious fanaticism a throwback to the medieval mentality.

RUSSIAN POGROMS

It has been the fate of the Jews—in century after century, nation after nation—to suffer killing and cruelty at the hands of Christians. Russia's turn in this savage cycle came in the late 1800s.

The czars, threatened by growing mutiny among peasants and workers, sought to divert the people's unrest by helping anti-Semitic groups rouse Orthodox hatred for Jews. Three waves of pogroms ensued: in the 1880s, just after the turn of the century, and during the Bolshevik Revolution. Each wave was increasingly murderous.

The first began when liberal Czar Alexander II was assassinated in 1882 by bomb-throwing nihilists. One of six rebels sentenced to death for the act happened to be a young Jewish woman, which brought dormant anti-Semitism surging to life. Mobs ravaged Jewish communities—mostly looting and beating, not killing. Severe anti-Jewish laws were passed, however, and Moscow's 35,000 Jews were expelled.

In 1903, as the First Russian Revolution was brewing, the czarist government—closely allied with the Orthodox hierarchy—aided the anti-Semitic press in attributing protests to "Jewish machinations." Marches and rallies were labeled "Jewish demonstrations" in an attempt to dissuade Orthodox Russians from joining the unrest. Lethal assaults on Jewish neighborhoods began—300 killed at Odessa, 120 at Yekaterinoslav, others in hundreds of villages. Later, it was discovered that pamphlets calling for pogroms had been printed on a press of the czarist secret police.

It was during the Bolshevik Revolution, however, that wholesale Jew-murder erupted. A few massacres were committed by the Red Army, under a slogan of "Strike at the bourgeoisie and the Jews." But most were done by the anti-Communist White Army and Ukrainian troops, who slaughtered thousands in Jewish towns as they passed. Altogether, 530 Jewish communities were attacked and about

60,000 Jews were killed.

On the surface, the pogroms weren't religious—yet they were rooted in the religious division of Russian society. The Orthodox faith bestrode the land, making a natural target of the vulnerable clusters of Jewish aliens, "different" people viewed with distrust, ready victims for pent-up anger of the majority.

ARMENIA

Human conflicts can be maddeningly complex, rooted in a tangle of religion, politics, language, nationalism, race, ethnicity, international power-grabbing, or other causes. That's how it was with one of history's little-known tragedies, the Armenian horror that killed more than one million Christians and Muslims during World War I.

Historically, Armenia—a tiny country on Turkey's northeast edge—was an enclave of Christians in a world of Muslims. It had been part of the Islamic Ottoman Empire since the 1300s and contained many followers of Mohammed. Strife between the two faiths was frequent. Orthodox Russia interfered repeatedly on the side of the Christians. (One such interference caused the Crimean War in

1854. The czar declared Russia the protector of Christians and holy places in Ottoman lands—and the sultan declared war.)

Late in the 1800s, Protestant missionaries began winning many converts in Armenia, creating a rivalry with entrenched Orthodox and Catholic groups. Out of the religious ferment grew a movement to create an independent Christian Armenia. The movement turned stormy in the 1890s. Protests turned into riots, which turned into massacres, which turned into armed combat. Some estimates say 200,000 Armenians were killed in the 1890s and 20,000 more in 1909.

The worst killing began in 1915, while the Ottoman Turks were involved in World War I on Germany's side. Christian Armenians, backed by Russia, rebelled against Turkey and began slaughtering Muslims. At Van they killed 30,000 and burned the Islamic part of the city. The Ottomans sent armies against the Armenians and forcibly relocated Armenian communities. The death toll was horrendous. After World War I ended, the Muslim-Christian killing continued until the 1920s, when Armenia was incorporated into the new Soviet Union.

Ever since, Armenian refugees around the

world have protested the murder of their nation, and to this day Armenian terrorists periodically assassinate Turkish officials.

However, some historians say that more Muslims than Christians died in the horror. Dr. Justin McCarthy of the University of Louisville estimates the 1915–1920 toll at 600,000 Armenians and 2.5 million Muslims. In 1985, when the House of Representatives passed a resolution condemning the Armenian genocide, McCarthy and sixty-eight other U.S. scholars took out a *New York Times* ad admonishing Congress:

"As for the charge of "genocide' . . . it cannot be viewed as separate from the suffering experienced by the Muslim inhabitants of the region. The weight of evidence so far uncovered points in the direction of serious inter-communal warfare (perpetrated by Muslim and Christian irregular forces) . . . not unlike the tragedy which has gone on in Lebanon for the past decade. The resulting death toll among both Muslim and Christian communities of the region was immense. . . ."

Finally, even under Soviet communism, Armenian religious clashes haven't ceased. In 1988, riots between Christian Armenians and neighboring Shi'ite Muslim Azerbaijanis killed more than a hundred and forced Soviet leaders to send in troops. The strife lasted eleven months, until a terrible earthquake struck Armenia.

THE HOLOCAUST

The most heinous butchery in human
history—the Nazi Holocaust—wasn't religious.

And yet it was.

For century after century after century,
the Christian church had designated the people
to be despised: the religious believers called
Jews, the "Christ-killers," the "enemies of God."
All the religious massacres of 900 years—by
Crusaders pursuing infidels, by inquisitors
hunting backsliders, by superstitious mobs
fearing tales of child-sacrificing, host-nailing,
and well-poisoning—branded Jews as accursed.
When popes ordered Jews to wear badges and
live in ghettos—or when they were expelled
entirely—it told the populace that these pariahs
were unfit to live among decent folk. Passion
plays depicting Jews as cruel mockers of Christ,

and cathedral paintings of the evil non-Christians, fanned hatred of those the church called "the perfidious Jews."

Thus, when Adolf Hitler needed a scapegoat group to rally the discontented majority to his cause and catapult himself to power, natural victims clearly marked by the church were at his disposal. The Christian public, not only in Germany but also throughout Europe, was predisposed to receive the Nazi message of Jew-hatred.

"The Holocaust was, of course, the bitter fruit of long centuries of Christian teaching about the Jewish people," wrote Dr. Franklin Littell, chairman of the religion department at Temple University. He urged study to "make it possible for persons of conscience to see where Christianity went wrong."

New York Times editor A. M. Rosenthal asked how, in the name of God, the Nazi nightmare could have occurred among educated modern people. "In the name of God?" he said. "It could not have been done had not the name of God been used for centuries to preach hatred of the Other, the Jews."

Theologian Clark Williamson of Christian Theological Seminary, Indianapolis, said centuries of Christian hostility to Jews

Grotesque-looking Jews were depicted as draining blood from innocent blonde children in this "blood libel" issue of the Nazi newspaper *Der Stürmer* in May, 1934.

"prepared the way for the Holocaust." He said the Nazis "are inconceivable apart from this Christian tradition. Hitler's pogrom, for all its distinctiveness, is the zenith of a long Christian heritage of teaching and practice against Jews."

For Christians, he said, the Holocaust demonstrated "the demonic results and malevolent possibilities that reside in our tradition of anti-Jewish preaching and teaching.

"Christian anti-Judaism promoted the Nazi cause in several ways. It led the Nazis to focus initially on Jews and created attitudes which permitted them to carry out their extermination program with little resistance. It made it possible for Christians to justify either assisting or not opposing the Nazi efforts. Christian anti-Judaism is profoundly incriminated in the Final Solution."

Theologian Richard Rubenstein wrote that the Nazis "did not invent a new villain. . . . They took over the 2,000-year-old Christian tradition of the Jew as villain. . . . The roots of the death camps must be sought in the mythic structure of Christianity. . . . Myths concerning the demonological role of the Jews have been operative in Christianity for centuries. . . ."

Jesuit theologian Peter de Rosa, who quit

Under Christmas wreaths, bodies of Jewish prisoners were stacked at the Buchenwald death camp in 1945. (Library of Congress print collection.)

the priesthood, lamented that Catholicism's "disastrous theology had prepared the way for Hitler and his 'final solution.' " He said his church published "over 100 anti-Semitic documents" through the centuries. "Not one conciliar decree, not one papal encyclical, bull, or pastoral directive suggests that Jesus's command, 'love your neighbor as yourself,' applied to Jews."

The bitter ex-Jesuit recounted in his 1988 book, *Vicars of Christ:* "Jews were hounded from one land to another. One pope gave them a month to quit their homes in Italy, leaving them only two places of refuge. During the Crusades, they were slaughtered in the thousands, out of devotion to Christ. A Jew who showed his nose on Good Friday was virtually committing suicide, even though the man on the cross had a Jewish nose. . . .

"There is, tragically, an undeniable link between . . . the papal legislation, the pogroms—and the gas chambers and crematoria of the Nazi death camps."

Researchers Paul Grosser and Edwin Halperin wrote: "If Nazi persecutions were not as 'Christian' as those perpetrated in the past, there was, certainly, an historic complicity. . . . By the time religious motivation and justification for anti-Semitism declined, the offshoots of that particular prejudice had already taken on a life of its own. . . . As a result, the Jews became the best-targeted prey for man's propensity to slander. . . ."

With the wrath of an Old Testament prophet, historian Dagobert Runes (whose mother was killed by the Nazis) blamed the Christian church for the Holocaust. He wrote:

"Everything Hitler did to the Jews, all the horrible, unspeakable misdeeds, had already been done to the smitten people before by the Christian churches. . . . The isolation of Jews into ghetto camps, the wearing of the yellow spot, the burning of Jewish books, and finally the burning of the people—Hitler learned it all from the church. However, the church burned Jewish women and children alive, while Hitler granted them a quicker death, choking them first with gas."

Dr. Runes said Christian priests and ministers still were inculcating hostility to Jews as the Third Reich arrived.

"The clergymen don't tell you whom to kill; they just tell you whom to hate," he wrote. "The Christian clergymen start teaching their young at the tenderest age that THE Jews killed the beloved, gentle Son of God; that God

Himself, the Father, punished THE Jews by dispersion and the burning of their holy city; that God holds THE Jews accursed forever. . . .

"For all the 2,000 years, there was no act of war against the Jews in which the church didn't play an intrinsic part. And wherever there was a trace of mercy, charity, or tolerance to be found amid this savagery, it came not from the church but from humanitarians in the civil world, as in Napoleonic France or during the American Revolution. . . .

"Some fancy that these brutal outrages . . . occurred only in the Dark Ages, as if this were an excuse. Nay, when George Washington was president, Jewish people were burning on the spit in Mexico. . . . Wherever there are Christian churches there is anti-Semitism."

When Nazism finally came, it was rooted in a fundamental fact: Religion had split Europe into a dominant majority and a vilified minority. Madmen rode this division to destruction.

Fifteen years after the ghastly contents of the death camps were revealed, reformer Pope John XXIII offered this prayer: "The mark of Cain is stamped upon our foreheads. Across the centuries, our brother Abel has lain in blood which we drew, and shed tears we caused by forgetting Thy love. Forgive us, Lord, for the curse we falsely attributed to their name as Jews."

INDIA

India has a unique word, *dharmiklarai*. It means "religious violence." The word is much needed in a tragic land cursed by never-ending hate between Hindus, Muslims, and Sikhs.

During the colonial era, when British guns held India captive, antipathy between the faiths was suppressed. It is profoundly ironic that one of history's great pacifists, Mohandas Gandhi, by finally succeeding in removing British control, inadvertently opened a floodgate of religious murder.

During the 1930s, when the Hindu Gandhi began winning concessions from the British rulers, India's Muslims felt excluded and demanded privileges. Lethal Muslim-Hindu riots broke out in many cities.

After World War II, as Britain prepared to

free the colony, disputes over Hindu and Muslim authority in the new government flared out of control. Rioting verged on anarchy. It was obvious that simple liberation would bring civil war. So, in 1947, Britain created two independent nations—India for Hindus and Pakistan for Muslims. But the partition didn't avert disaster.

Hindus living in Pakistan began a massive exodus to India, and Muslims in India did the opposite. In the single month of September 1947, more than 4 million migrants crossed the border. Religious hate between passing processions exploded in massacres. The dharmiklarai spread to many cities, wreaking death and destruction. In the Kashmir and Junagadh provinces, military combat broke out. The death toll during the partition is estimated as high as 1 million. Gandhi himself was killed by a Hindu who thought him too pro-Muslim.

Ever since, religious murder has been recurring. Trifles cause dormant hostility to flare.

In 1980, more than 200 were killed in the Moradabad region because a pig walked through a Muslim holy ground. Muslims accused Hindus of driving the "unclean" animal into their sacred spot, and a wave of riots ensued.

An unidentified militant Sikh gently coaches a three-year-old Sikh child how to aim a pistol inside the complex of the ornate Golden Temple. The Sikh agitation claimed at least 735 lives in 1988. (AP, April 20, 1988.)

In 1983, in the northeastern Assam province, more than 2,000 were killed in Hindu-Muslim clashes.

In 1984, near Bombay, a Hindu leader made an anti-Islam speech and Muslims retaliated by hanging dirty sandals on his portrait, a religious insult. Soon mobs were in the streets with knives, guns, spears, and firebombs. A week of arson riots left 216 dead, 756 wounded, 13,000 homeless, and 4,100 under arrest.

In 1989 a Muslim religious procession at Indore was startled by the sound of a nearby explosion. The marchers attacked Hindus in the vicinity, triggering a pitched battle with guns, rocks, and pipes. Shops and cars were set afire. At least fifteen were killed and seventy-five injured. Also in 1989, more than 300 believers killed each other in northern India because of a holy-ground dispute at Ayodhya. Hindus attempted to build a temple on the spot where they think Lord Rama was born, but Muslims refused to remove a mosque from the site. Murderous violence ensued, with roving bands of Hindus torching Muslim homes.

India's greatest horror in the 1980s stemmed from attempts by Sikhs to create an independent theocracy—Khalistan, "land of the

An unidentified man killed by the crossfire between Sikh militants and paramilitary police lay outside the Golden Temple complex as the police continued the seige for a third day. At least ten people were killed according to the authorities. (AP, May 11, 1988.)

pure"—in the Punjab region. Many followed a fundamentalist preacher, Jarnail Bhindranwale, who taught that Sikhs have "a religious duty to send opponents to hell." They began a terror campaign, systematically killing unarmed Hindu families.

In 1984, the extremists barricaded themselves in their holiest shrine, the Golden Temple at Amritsar, while colleagues outside continued terrorism. Prime Minister Indira Gandhi sent troops to free the temple, and 1,000 died in the fighting, including Bhindranwale. Then Sikhs among Gandhi's personal guard assassinated her with a fusillade of fifty shots. Her death sent India's Hindus on a vengeance rampage that killed 5,000 Sikhs in three days. Mobs dragged Sikhs from homes, stores, buses, and trains, slashing and pounding them to death. Some were doused with kerosene and burned alive. Sikh boys were castrated.

Sikh terrorism didn't cease. Bombs were planted on Air India jetliners and random killings of defenseless Hindus continued. During the first five months of 1988, extremists killed 1,168 in ambushes of Hindu weddings, holy festivals, and family gatherings. They seized the Golden Temple again. They

killed at least 300 moderate Sikhs who
disagreed with the strategy of employing
murder to establish "the land of the pure."

SUDAN

Africa's largest nation, the Republic of the Sudan, became the second country to plunge into a religious bloodbath after British military rulers departed.

Ever since the 1890s, when the self-proclaimed Mahdi, "the Divinely Guided One," caused ghastly religious warfare, the British had governed the Sudan and kept the peace. Finally, Britain agreed to free the country in 1956—setting the stage for conflict between part-Arab Muslims of the north and Christian and animist tribes of the south.

The southerners feared that the northern majority would impose Islamic strictures upon them. They began rebelling in 1955, even before the British withdrew. The outbreaks turned into a holy war that raged for seventeen years, killing an estimated 500,000 civilians and leaving 750,000 homeless. A truce finally was achieved in 1972.

Then in 1983, it began all over again— largely because President Gaafar Muhammad al-Nimeiry subjected the whole country to harsh Islamic religious law, the *shari'a*, which mandates that thieves shall have their hands or feet chopped off, that unmarried lovers shall be stoned to death, and that other offenders shall be flogged.

During the next eighteen months, 400 thieves were axed with ceremonial swords. The pathetic cripples began begging in dusty streets. International revulsion rose. The United States State Department declared that Sudan's imposition of Islamic law on Christians was a violation of human rights, and that the amputations were a cruel and unusual punishment.

Even some Muslims protested. Mahmoud Mohammed Taha, head of a sect called the Republican Brothers, called for the repeal of *shari'a*. He was convicted of heresy and hanged in 1985 before a chanting crowd of 2,000 Muslims. His sect was outlawed.

The *shari'a* punishments produced grotesque scenes. "Amputation days" were advertised in newspapers, drawing large crowds to Kober Prison in Khartoum. The audience chanted Islamic slogans while prison attendants waved aloft severed hands and feet. Possession of alcohol was punishable by flogging—and one visiting Italian Catholic priest was beaten in public for having sacramental wine.

Islamic police patrols at roadblocks watched for adulterers. Married couples began keeping their wedding documents in their cars to avoid detainment. Some men traveling with their teen-age daughters carried the girls' birth certificates to avoid accusations of adultery.

Imposition of *shari'a* sent the south's Christians and animists back into full revolt. The death toll to civilians was horrible. The Christian-led rebel army often captured villages and confiscated all food, leaving the inhabitants to starve. Then government Muslim troops recaptured the villages and burned them to the ground.

In 1985, Nimeiry was ousted and replaced by Sadiq al-Mahdi, a great-grandson of the historic Mahdi. The new Mahdi promised to abolish *shari'a*, but hard-line Muslims in the government refused.

The civil war worsened. In 1988, Mahdi

ordered UNICEF to stop shipping food and medicine to the ravished south. Relief workers estimated that 250,000 southern Sudanese starved to death in 1988.

In 1989, Mahdi was ousted and thrown into prison with his cabinet. New leader Omar el Bashir once again promised repeal of *shari'a* and begged for a halt in the fighting.

During twenty-four years, the recurring religious war in Sudan has killed more than a million people.

ULSTER

A deadly mixture of religion, politics, and nationalism has made Northern Ireland one of the most hate-plagued lands in the world.

It's a place where Catholic and Protestant terrorists endlessly kill each other, and kill peacekeeping police, and kill civilians who get in the way or speak out too forcefully. Catholics suspected of disloyalty to the Catholic cause are "kneecapped" by pistol shots.

It's a place where working-class Catholics and Protestants live in guarded neighborhoods, afraid to venture into "enemy territory," afraid for their children to be far from home. Twenty-foot-high "peace walls" separate religious sectors, blocking sniper bullets but not high-flung rocks and firebombs.

How did Ulster, as Ireland's north is

known, become a horror spot? The answer is rooted in four centuries of complex religio-political conflict involving the whole island of Ireland.

Even in olden times, when England was Catholic, it had sought to subjugate Ireland, with marginal success. When Henry VIII created Anglican Protestantism, he also assumed the title of king of Ireland and attempted to impose his new religion there—thus starting interminable religious mutinies. Elizabeth I crushed Catholic uprisings and completed the conquest of Ireland.

Then James I radically changed the northern Ulster district by seizing Catholic lands and giving them to Protestants from Scotland and England. The ousted Catholics starved in the hills. Some finally crept back, begging for field jobs on their former farms. They became a bitter minority in Ulster.

Throughout Ireland, continued Catholic upheavals incurred British reprisals such as the onslaught of Cromwell's Puritan army. Under the Penal Laws in the 1700s, Catholicism was outlawed and all priests were banished. Catholics who persisted in secret worship in the forests were hunted with bloodhounds and often killed. Catholics eventually were

The scene of devastation in Rotten Row, London, after an IRA bomb attack on the Household Cavalry killed four soldiers and seven of their horses. (AP, July 20, 1982.)

emancipated in the 1800s, but they were forced to pay tithes to the Anglican Church. This triggered the fitful Tithe War in which both sides perpetrated cruelties.

The strife continued until finally, in the 20th century, southern Ireland was liberated as an independent nation, 95 percent Catholic. But Ulster Protestants—descendants of the usurpers of Catholic lands—feared being swallowed in a "popish" unified Ireland. They voted to remain part of Great Britain. That brought on the modern nightmare between Ulster's Protestants and Catholics.

In the 1950s, the clandestine Catholic paramilitary Irish Republican Army waged terrorism in Ulster in an attempt to force unification with the south. In 1962, the IRA renounced killing, but random violence continued.

In 1968 and 1969, poor Catholics excluded from Ulster's economy staged riots. Protestant militants responded with guns, bombs, and burning. Then the IRA's Provisional wing—the fanatical "Provos"—countered with escalated killing. The British army was called in. Barricades, guard posts, and barbed wire divided Ulster into religious compounds.

Bloodshed was worst in the 1970s, after

which it settled to a steady pace, For example, in 1985, a quiet year, there were fifty-four assassinations, 148 bombings, 237 shooting episodes, 916 woundings, thirty-one kneecappings, 522 arrests on terrorism charges, and 3.3 tons of explosives and weapons seized. All this in a tiny country with a population of 1.5 million people.

The havoc is caused by four known terrorist groups—and some not known. For example, gunmen burst into a Protestant church at Darkley in 1983 and used automatic weapons on worshipers, killing three and wounding seven. Later, the unfamiliar "Catholic Reaction Force" took credit for the act.

Hatred prevails. At "interface streets" where Catholic and Protestant neighborhoods touch, police vigilance is necessary to prevent assaults. And the police must wear armor. Homes on each side of the "peace walls" are scarred from projectiles.

Protestant extremists are epitomized by the demagogic, theatrical Rev. Ian Paisley, a member of both the British and European parliaments, who created his own Free Presbyterian Church to fight Catholicism. He rants that "the Church of Rome" isn't

Christian, and calls the Catholic mass "a blasphemy and a deceit." He sneers at "bachelor priests" and "idolatrous worship." From the other side, Catholics won't let their children attend "mixed" schools.

Attempts to heal the hate are futile. A Protestant minister, the Rev. David Armstrong, made a goodwill visit to a nearby Catholic congregation. Soon he suffered a near-riot in his congregation and was forced to leave Ireland. Some Protestants and Catholics jointly formed the Alliance Party in an attempt to "detribalize" Ulster, but they get few votes. Two women, one Catholic and one Protestant, won the 1976 Nobel Peace Prize for their doomed attempt at reconciliation.

By 1990 the death toll from the latest two decades of Ulster's hostilities was near 3,000.

JONESTOWN

A religious horror unlike any other astonished the world in 1978.

More than 900 members of an American church colony committed mass suicide, after the colony's armed guards killed visiting examiners.

The disaster was caused by a lone minister, the Reverend Jim Jones. As a young idealist in Indiana, he founded the Peoples Temple, a mixed-race congregation of poor people. He provided a soup kitchen for the needy, a nursing home for the elderly, and a used-clothing supply for the threadbare. Jones led efforts to halt racial segregation in restaurants and theaters. In 1961 he became head of the Indianapolis Human Rights Commission.

Odd reports began emerging from the Peoples Temple. Jones proclaimed himself a prophet of God, then Jesus himself. To prove it, he performed miracles: removing cancers and conducting other forms of faith-healing. Skeptics said the "cancers" were chicken livers. Jones went to Brazil briefly as a missionary. In 1964 he was ordained by the Disciples of Christ. He preached that the world would end on July 15, 1967. It didn't.

Jones read a magazine article listing places that would be safest from radioactive fallout after a nuclear war. One was Ukiah, California. He loaded up 150 of his followers and moved to rural Ukiah. The Peoples Temple boomed; membership grew to 5,000. The Temple moved again in 1971 to a black section of San Francisco. It offered a free-dining hall, a drug rehabilitation program, a free clinic, a legal-aid office, a day-care center, and a senior citizen center. Jones claimed 20,000 followers.

Political figures flocked to Jones. Former Governor Jerry Brown, the late Mayor George Moscone, and even actress Jane Fonda shared the podium with him. Moscone appointed Jones chairman of the San Francisco Housing Authority. Politicians knew that Peoples Temple members were potent on election day.

This scene from the 1978 Jonestown tragedy shows the liquid death potion and the victims who drank it. Two years after the People's Temple massacre, Jonestown was a ghost town, with a dozen guards and workers keeping out the curious and the jungle vegetation. (AP, Nov. 18, 1980.)

But the ugly side of Jones's ministry grew. Rumors circulated that children were beaten, that weird sexual activity was taking place, that adults were required to give all their assets and their welfare checks to the church, that the minister led his flock in suicide drills. Jones and many followers began spending much of their time at Jonestown, a farm colony the Peoples Temple had acquired in Guyana, South America.

In 1977, *New West* magazine published reports from former members exposing abuses in the Peoples Temple. They said many members wanted to leave but were afraid to go. Two who quit, Jeannie and Al Mills, published a bitter book, *Six Years with God*. In early 1978, more than fifty relatives of Jonestown residents asked Secretary of State Cyrus Vance to help remove their family members from the "concentration camp." Congressmen were petitioned.

In November, 1978, Rep. Leo Ryan of California flew to Jonestown to check on the complaints. He took with him several aides, news reporters, State Department officers, and relatives of colonists. They landed at an airstrip at a Guyanese town near the colony. They were shown hospitably around the settlement,

Bodies of the religious cult, The People's Temple, surround the meeting hall in Jonestown, Guyana. Some 914 bodies were recovered by a team of U.S. soldiers. (AP, Nov. 26, 1978.)

and all seemed well.

The second day, the mood changed. A colony member slipped a television reporter a note begging for help in leaving Jonestown. A man with a knife tried to attack Rep. Ryan. The visitors decided to leave. Sixteen colonists asked to go with them. They all rode in a truck to the airstrip. As they boarded two planes, one of the defectors, a stooge sent by Jones, pulled a pistol and began shooting into the group. Then three gunmen appeared, took guns from a trailer and began firing. Ryan was wounded. So were two NBC News reporters and a *San Francisco Examiner* reporter. Then all four were executed with point-blank bullets in the head. A woman defector from the colony also was killed. Eleven others were wounded. The rest fled into the jungle or were left unhurt as the killers sped off to avoid nearby Guyanese soldiers.

Back at the settlement, Jones assembled his followers and announced that the congressman's party had been executed. He said it was time "for us to meet in another place." The believers gave a clenched-fist salute. Guards with automatic rifles ringed the area.

The camp's physician and two nurses mixed cyanide with fruit drink in a steel drum. The colonists lined up for doses of death. The fluid was squirted into the mouths of babies. The victims fell in random rows while Jones kept talking into the public address system and chanting "mother, mother, mother." His body later was found with a bullet wound in the head. Only two other colonists were shot. Altogether, 914 died. Nearly 300 of them were children. A handful of members slipped into the jungle and survived.

The Peoples Temple maintained a headquarters in Georgetown, Guyana's capital. On the day of the mass suicide, a woman leader at the Georgetown office and her three children had their throats cut.

In the aftermath, authorities found $10 million of Peoples Temple wealth hoarded in banks in Panama and elsewhere.

More than a year later, Jeannie and Al Mills, who had spearheaded the exposure of Peoples Temple evils, were killed by shots in the head at their California home, along with their 15-year-old daughter.

A *Newsweek* commentary said the tragedy "shows how easily saintliness and faith can turn into insanity and mass hysteria."

LEBANON

Religious tribalism—segregation of a society into sectarian camps—produced a horrible result in Lebanon.

The once-lovely nation was laid waste by endless, senseless slaughter between Sunni Muslims, Shi'ite Muslims, Druze Muslims, Alawite Muslims, Maronite Christians—plus Jews from neighboring Israel. For at least fifteen years, daily news reports were filled with accounts of "Christian snipers" and "Shi'ite militia attacks" and "Druze machine-gunners" and "Sunni suicide bombers" and the like. The death toll has passed 130,000, and there is no end in sight.

Lebanon's tragedy stemmed from intertwined Mideast social and political stresses. Underlying the chaos was the basic fact that

Lebanese groups are more loyal to their faiths than to their nation. When former French governors departed in 1946, power-sharing was arranged among Lebanon's religions: the new government always would have a Maronite Christian president, a Sunni Muslim prime minister, and a Shi'ite Muslim speaker of parliament.

The power-sharing worked, guardedly, until 1975. Then violence erupted between Christians and Muslims, and the many groups took up weapons. After visiting the torn land, journalist Mark Patinkin wrote: "Lebanon split by faith. Religions began to form militias. And imagine what hatreds would grow in America if the Protestants formed an army, and then the Catholics, and then the Jews, each arming themselves not merely with handguns but with artillery?" Combat flared and subsided and flared again, time after time, year after year. Various militias controlled their own neighborhoods or villages. They repeatedly formed alliances, then turned on each other. At least ten different armed groups joined in the fighting:

(1) Hezbollah, the Party of God, a Shi'ite faction linked to Iran, (2) the Amal militia, composed of Shi'ites linked to Syria, (3) the

Tawheed fundamentalist Sunni militia, (4) the Alawite Arab Democratic Party, (5) the Druze Progressive Socialist Party, (6) the Lebanese national army, composed chiefly of Maronite Christians, (7) the Lebanese Forces, a rival Christian group linked to the Phalangist Party, (8) the Syrian army, which first entered Lebanon as a peacekeeping force, (9) fighters of Palestinian refugees in Lebanon, (10) the Islamic Jihad, a shadowy Shi'ite terrorist group. In addition, the Israeli army has invaded Lebanon twice, and the United States, France, and the United Nations have sent peacekeeping troops.

Helpless civilians fell victim as the religious militias fired furious fusillades. Snipers of several faiths picked off travelers crossing the "Green Line" dividing Beirut's Christian and Muslim sectors. Car bombs regularly exploded in one sector or the other, shattering and maiming civilians. After bombings, witnesses told of blood spattered as high as the third floors of shattered office buildings. Westerners were kidnaped or executed by Muslim factions. One group videotaped the hanging of a United Nations employee, while a crowd chanted: "God is great. Long live Islam."

Death is welcomed by some Muslim

fighters—such as the suicide bombers who drove an explosives-laden truck into the United States Marine barracks at Beirut Airport in 1983, killing 241 servicemen. The military chief of the Amal Shi'ite militia told a TV news interviewer:

"None of us is afraid. God is with us and gives us strength. We are making a race like horses to see who goes to God first. I want to die before my friends. They want to die before me. We want to see our God."

And Amal is generally considered less fanatical than its Shi'ite rival, Hezbollah, the Party of God.

Some of the Muslim fighters call themselves "Salabeyeen"—the name of Saladin's Muslim warriors who fought Christian Crusaders in the 12th century.

In 1985, four Soviet Embassy employees were kidnapped in Beirut, evidently by Sunni fundamentalist Tawheed members angered because Soviet weapons were being used against them by rival Islamic militias. One Russian's body was later dumped by a sports arena with a close-range bullet wound in the head. A caller told news bureaus: "We have carried out God's sentence against one of the hostages." The other three Russians eventually were released as a "goodwill gesture." Afterward, a Rand Corporation terrorism expert, Brian Jenkins, commented that religion magnifies Mideast violence. "As we have seen throughout history," he said, "the presumed approval of God for the killing of pagans, heathens, or infidels can permit great acts of destruction and self-destruction."

Analysts are at a loss to explain the hatreds that propel Lebanon's religious factions. The word "madness" is frequently used. Nobel Prize-winning author Isaac Bashevis Singer, speaking of humankind in general, observed:

"I live in a kind of fear and despair all the time. I read the newspaper every day and see what people are doing to one another, how they kill or provoke others to kill. In Lebanon, for example, there is a rage that has taken over the whole population. Everybody hates and is ready to kill everybody else. Sometimes I am afraid that Lebanon is an indication of what may happen to the whole of humanity. Something will break out—a revolution, a counterrevolution—and people will just drink one another's blood."

IRAN

Religion gained absolute sway in Iran in 1979, and it produced a government of startling cruelty.

Iran's fundamentalist Shi'ite theocracy has become a symbol of inhumanity. It has applied the death penalty more freely than any other regime in the world. Morals squads patrol the streets, hunting impiety. Hate slogans fill the public scene. Women are forced into shrouded subjugation. It is as if evil, rather than religion, has taken control.

In former times, Iran under the shahs wasn't a democratic paradise. Corrupt rulers used the Savak secret police to suppress unrest. There was plenty of it to suppress, because Shah Muhammad Riza Pahlavi sought to westernize the country, and conservative

Shi'ite mullahs cried heresy. These holy men wanted a return to harsh Islamic law. Much of the populace agreed.

The most strident mullah, the Ayatollah Khomeini, who had been banished to France, directed the growing revolt from afar. The climax came in 1979 when the shah fled and Khomeini returned in triumph to establish "the government of God on earth." The nature of "God's government" quickly became apparent to the world. While the dying shah was in an American hospital, a top Iranian cleric commanded: "I order all students and Muslims in the United States, including Africans, Filipinos, and Palestinians, to drag him out of the hospital and dismember him."

Iran's clergy took power in parliament and passed rigid Islamic laws. Khomeini warned dissenters: "If you do not obey, you will be annihilated." Moderates were removed swiftly. Liberal President Abolhassan Bani-Sadr was deposed and exiled. Foreign Minister Sadegh Ghotbzadeh was sent to a firing squad. Before his death, he smuggled a note from prison apologizing to the world for having supported "the satanic regime of the mullahs."

Torture and executions became rampant. Foreign diplomats living near a detention center

Baha'is have suffered ugly persecution in Iran during the 1980s at the hands of Shi'ite Muslims. Above, Muslims destroy the House of the Bab, the most sacred Baha'i spot in Iran. Below is seventeen-year-old Mona Mahmudnzhad of Shiraz, one of many Baha'is hanged by the theocracy because she would not convert to Islam. (Photos courtesy of Baha'i Office of Public Information, Wilmette, Ill.)

in Teheran said their nights were tormented by
unbearable screams and frequent gunshots. By
1983, Amnesty International, the worldwide
human-rights organization, counted reports of
5,195 executions in the first four years of the
religious regime. The "60 Minutes" news show
reported that, because Islamic law forbids
execution of virgins, some condemned young
women were raped by guards before being
shot. Also, Amnesty International said some
Iranians were being killed or mutilated under
the Islamic "law of retaliation," which allows
crime victims to inflict their own punishments
on offenders.

The most purely religious killing was the
mass execution of Baha'is who refused to
convert to Islam. Groups including women and
teen-agers were hanged in public. Fugitive
Baha'is who escaped to other nations brought
photos of the carnage. The United States
Committee for Refugees quoted an Iranian
Shi'ite judge as justifying the killings on the
basis of a Koran prayer: "Lord, leave not a
single family of infidels on the Earth."

When Iraq invaded an edge of Iran, the
fierce-eyed ayatollah responded with frenzied
warfare that sent hundreds of thousands of
ill-trained young Iranians to die in human-wave

charges. In December 1984, on Mohammed's birthday, Khomeini told his people:

"War is a blessing for the world and for all nations. It is God who incites men to fight and to kill. The Koran says, 'Fight until all corruption and all rebellion have ceased.' The wars the Prophet led against the infidels were a blessing for all humanity. Imagine that we soon will win the war. That will not be enough, for corruption and resistance to Islam will still exist. The Koran says, 'War, war until victory.' . . . The mullahs with corrupt hearts who say that all this is contrary to the teachings of the Koran are unworthy of Islam. Thanks to God, our young people are now, to the limits of their means, putting God's commandments into action. They know that to kill the unbelievers is one of man's greatest missions."

Amid all the killing, Iran also declared war on sexuality. Women were commanded to shroud themselves so completely that no lock of hair showed. Morality patrols in white jeeps cruised streets, arresting women for being "badly veiled" and sending them to prison camps for three-month rehabilitation courses. Western magazines entering Iran went first to censors who laboriously blacked out every woman's picture except for her eyes. Women were allowed to swim and ski—but only in shrouds, and only at segregated beaches and slopes.

Executions multiplied. Amnesty International said 1,466 Iranians were put to death in the first nine months of 1989. Some of the victims were women charged with prostitution. Amnesty added that seventy-eight Iranians had been stoned to death, mostly for sexual transgressions, and others had their hands chopped off under Islamic law.

All these internal cruelties of the religious government drew minor notice around the world—but one of the Ayatollah Khomeini's acts jolted the West. He commanded faithful Muslims to assassinate a "blaspheming" British author who had hinted that Mohammed's revelations in the Koran didn't come from heaven. The writer, Salman Rushdie, went into hiding. Many Western governments curtailed diplomatic relations with Iran.

The ayatollah died in 1989. His call for Rushdie's assassination may be remembered as his most controversial act. But, in truth, it was the least of his evils.

MUSLIM GORE

In addition to the religious horrors in Iran, Lebanon, Sudan, and India, sporadic Muslim killing has scarred many nations in the 1980s. Much of it has been caused by Shi'ites inflamed by the triumph of the Shi'ite uprising in Iran. Other episodes had other origins. Here's a country-by-country record:

Saudia Arabia

In Saudi Arabia, the new wave of Muslim gore involved both Shi'ites and Sunnis.

Although the Wahhabi kingdom leads the world in Islamic strictness—with women in shrouds, polygamy ordained by law, and holiness a daily presence—another "Mahdi" arose to "cleanse" Saudi Arabia of worldliness. He was a Sunni named Juhaiman al Otaiba. He was a student of Sheikh Abdel al Baz, the absolutist rector of the University of Medina. (The sheikh once wrote a paper denouncing the Copernican "heresy" and maintaining that the sun orbits the earth. He also said the Earth is flat and that NASA's moon landings were faked.) Juhaiman, the new Mahdi, demanded expulsion of all non-Muslims, abolition of television, and a halt to the education of women.

On November 20, 1979, Juhaiman used automatic weapons as holy instruments. While 40,000 pilgrims were assembled at the Grand Mosque in Mecca for the yearly *hajj*, the return to Islam's holiest shrine, Juhaiman and more than 200 armed followers fired briefly, killed an acolyte, and seized the mosque. Over loudspeakers, they proclaimed that a messiah had arrived. The 40,000 pilgrims were told to join the new order or leave. "The takeover was as shocking and unexpected to Muslims as a forcible seizure of the Vatican would be to the Catholic world," Mideast correspondent Robin Wright wrote in her book, *Sacred Rage*.

Five days later, after Wahhabi holy men gave permission for the government to use weapons in the mosque, 2,000 troops were sent in. Nine days of room-to-room fighting ensued. In the end, 255 soldiers, fanatics, and pilgrims were killed, and twice as many were wounded. Juhaiman and 170 followers were captured. They were tried in a secret religious court. Minor participants were sentenced to prison, and sixty-three leaders were ordered beheaded with ceremonial, decorated swords. The decapitations were spread among eight cities for maximum public impact.

Meanwhile, on the opposite side of Saudi Arabia, a Shi'ite upheaval occurred. The Wahhabi government had forbidden Shi'ites to engage in their gory custom of beating themselves bloody during the festival of Ashura, which commemorates the martyrdom of Mohammed's grandson Hussein. But in 1979, Shi'ites defied the ban and began self-flagellation. Police moved in. Crowds rioted, smashing stores and burning cars. At least seventeen Shi'ites were killed. Then 20,000 national troops, mostly Sunnis, were sent in. Deadly clashes took more lives.

Through the 1980s, violence had broken out among delegations of Muslims gathered in Mecca for the yearly *hajj*. In 1987, more than 400 were killed in rioting triggered by Iranian

Shi'ites. In 1989, Shi'ite terrorists detonated bombs near the Grand Mosque during the *hajj*, killing one pilgrim and wounding sixteen. Later, a religious court convicted sixteen Kuwaiti fanatics for the attack, and they were publicly beheaded with swords in Mecca.

Egypt

In Egypt, religious fanaticism and conflict rose in 1980. Some of it involved Coptic Christians. Some involved Muslims of the *Al Jihad* clique, which planted bombs in Coptic churches. Most of it involved Sunni extremists in the Muslim Brotherhood, who deemed President Anwar Sadat a religious traitor because he signed the Camp David Treaty recognizing Israel.

In 1981, as the religious ferment grew more dangerous, Sadat ordered a crackdown. Police detained 1,600 Sunni and Coptic militants. Fifteen extreme Islamic societies were outlawed. Radical Muslim publications were banned. The Coptic pope was exiled to a desert monastery, and the chief of the Muslim Brotherhood was imprisoned.

Then on October 6, 1981, while Sadat was reviewing a military parade, a group of Muslim fanatics in the army leaped from the procession and killed him with grenades and rifles. At their trial, the leader said he was proud of the assassination "because the cause of religion was at stake." He said he was "at the peak of joy" because he soon would join God. Introduced as evidence at the trial was an *Al Jihad* handbook calling on members to "uproot the infidel leadership" and telling them that "the peak of worship is jihad."

(Ironically, the assassins had been careful not to violate Islamic religious law. Wanting money to buy guns, they had asked theologian Omar Rahman to issue a *fatwa*, a religious edict, saying it was permissible to rob a Christian jewelry store in Cairo to finance the holy purpose.)

Two days after Sadat's murder, Muslim fundamentalists in Asyut south of Cairo stormed a police station and killed a number of officers. Troops were sent in. Deaths in the fighting reached eighty-seven. Hundreds of religious militants later were convicted in a mass trial.

Fundamentalism grew ominously in Egypt in the 1980s, causing frequent clashes with police. Crowds demanded an Islamic government ruled by the *shari'a* religious law. In 1987, Muslims attacked Coptic Christians

because of a rumor that a Coptic secret spray
caused crosses to appear on Muslim women's
veils. The government banned religious
bumper stickers on cars because they triggered
street clashes popularly called "the bumper
sticker war." In 1989, rioting caused the arrest
of 1,500 Muslim militants. Holy man Rahman
called for the assassination of Nobel
Prize-winning author Naguib Mahfouz on
grounds that one of his books insulted Islam.

Syria

In Syria, members of the Sunni fundamentalist
Muslim Brotherhood began an uprising at
Hama in 1982, killing local government officials
and their families. Alawite Muslim President
Hafez Assad reacted with horrible vengeance.
He sent in tank-led army units that destroyed
the city, killing an estimated 20,000 people.
Mass executions were held. A rebel section of
the city was bulldozed. In retaliation, a Muslim
Brotherhood suicide bomber shattered the
Information Ministry in Damascus.

The following year, Mufti Sheikh Sa'ad
e-Din el'Alami of Jerusalem issued a *fatwa*
promising "a place in Paradise for eternity" to

any Islamic martyr who would kill the "infidel" President Assad.

The destruction of Hama was cited by Mideast correspondent Thomas Friedman in his book *From Beirut to Jerusalem*. He said the Muslim world's religio-political conflict is conducted according to "Hama Rules"—"and Hama rules are no rules at all."

Kuwait

In Kuwait, growing fundamentalist pressure reached a climax in 1983 when Shi'ites blew up several facilities. The plotters were caught because, in the debris of a suicide bombing, police found the bomber's thumb, and the thumbprint helped identify the group. Six of the fanatics were sentenced to death and fourteen were imprisoned. Meanwhile, other Shi'ites hijacked a Kuwaiti airliner in 1984, forced it to land in Teheran, and began killing Americans aboard it, in a futile attempt to win release of Kuwait's religious bombers. After one American's body was thrown out, the killers announced: "The reason for our action was for the pleasure of God and secondly to help our innocent brothers."

Afghanistan

In Afghanistan, the civil war that enmeshed the
Soviet army through the 1980s and caused
more than 1 million deaths was largely a
religious rebellion by Muslims opposing
Westernization. The *mujahideen* (holy warriors)
were attacking not only their communist
government but also modern life. Here's an
illustration related by Steven Galster, author of
a book on the war: "In March 1979, before the
Soviet military intervention, the Afghan
government's literacy campaign for women
encountered strong resistance from mullahs
and other conservative elements in the western
city of Herat. Demonstrations culminated in a
revolt in which several Afghan officials and
Soviet advisers were slaughtered, cut to pieces,
and paraded around the city." A BBC
documentary in 1986 featured a rebel leader of
the National Islamic Front who said he had
sentenced between 6,000 and 7,000 prisoners
of war to death. (A different rebel group,
Hezb-i-Islami, denounced the BBC as "the voice
of the demon.")

Reporter John Fullerton, in his book *The
Soviet Occupation of Afghanistan*, described this
treatment of captured Russians: "One group

was killed, skinned, and hung up in a butcher's shop. One captive found himself the center of attraction in a game of buzkashi, that rough-and-tumble form of Afghan polo in which a headless goat is usually the ball. The captive was used instead. Alive. He was literally torn to pieces."

Soviet atrocities in Afghanistan were widely reported, but those of the Muslim rebels drew little notice. Asia Watch reported in 1989 that *mujahideen* and Wahhabi Arab volunteers captured a city in Kunar province, then ravaged it in a spree of killing, looting and raping. Although America's CIA smuggled $2 billion worth of weapons to the rebels, to undercut the Soviet Union, the Muslims hardly were U.S. allies. American columnist Richard Reeves observed: "Fundamentally, the *mujahideen* see us as no different from Russians. We, the communists and the democrats, are both modernizers. And it is modernism that the warriors of Allah are fighting. Most of them will turn on us in a moment if we advocate the same godless reforms as those initiated by the Soviet invaders—especially the modern reform the Afghan fighters hate most, the education of women."

Nigeria

In Nigeria, several Muslim groups engaged in murderous uprisings. One sect led by Mallam Marwa stormed the old walled city of Kano in 1980 in a clash that killed 400, including Marwa. In 1982 his followers, called heretics by other Muslims, seized the city of Maiduguri and began killing "infidels." When the militia arrived, the fanatics sprinkled themselves with magical powder to make them impervious to police bullets. It didn't work. After four days of battling, more than 1,000 were dead, including the fanatics. Another Muslim-versus-Muslim clash in 1985 at Gombe killed 100.

In 1987 a Muslim woman slapped a Christian evangelist at Kafanchan, saying he had insulted Islam. Riots broke out in several cities, causing dozens of deaths and the burning of hundreds of churches. The government banned open-air preaching.

Elsewhere

In Bahrain, a group of Shi'ite fanatics plotted in 1981 to seize the tiny Persian Gulf sheikhdom, but the conspiracy was discovered and stopped.

A total of seventy-three Shi'ites were convicted and imprisoned.

In Tunisia, terrorists of the Islamic Tendency Movement were imprisoned in 1987 for bombing hotels. In the Philippines, armed Muslim squads rule certain territories. In Indonesia, combat between Muslim militants and police in 1989 killed thirty-two. In Soviet Uzbekistan, rioting between Sunni and Shi'ite believers in 1989 caused more than a hundred deaths. In Israel, the government banned fundamentalist Muslim organizations, adding fuel to Palestinian protests.

Meanwhile, the grim *shari'a* Islamic religious law was applied in several Muslim lands. In Pakistan in 1987, a 25-year-old carpenter's daughter was sentenced to be stoned to death for having unmarried sex. In Saudi Arabia in 1977, a teen-age princess and her lover were executed in public. In the United Arab Emirates in 1984, a cook and a maid were sentenced to stoning for adultery—but, as a show of mercy, the execution was postponed until after the maid's baby was born.

A FORCE FOR GOOD?

Religion is a word with so many meanings that it nearly defies definition.

It means Appalachian snake-handlers dying of rattlesnake bites because the Bible commands believers to "take up serpents."

It means Mother Teresa feeding and clothing the poor of Calcutta.

It means Hindu Tamils and Buddhists killing each other in ambushes on the island of Sri Lanka.

It means Witness for Peace volunteers living and working in Nicaraguan villages so their presence will shield peasants from guerrilla attacks.

It means "cargo cult" believers in New Guinea prayerfully waiting for airplanes to come to them.

It means Albert Schweitzer spending his life treating sick Africans.

It means twenty-five years of armed stand-off between Muslims and Orthodox Christians on the island of Cyprus.

Religion encompasses everything from whirling dervishes to Oxford theologians, from Pentecostals spouting the "unknown tongue" to Bishop Desmond Tutu receiving the Nobel Prize. Hindus worship thousands of gods, including Shiva's erect penis—while many Unitarian-Universalists are godless agnostics. And there were hundreds of faiths that died: the once-intense worship of Zeus, Jupiter, Baal, Molech, Adonis, Ra, Isis, and a host of other gods. Religion has a thousand contradictory faces—yet they're *all* religion.

By numbers, contemporary religion is more than a matter of 1.6 billion Christians or 900 million Muslims or 700 million Hindus. Anthropologists say a little-known major faith is the tribal spirit-worshipers, shamanists, animists, and other magic-believers of the undeveloped world.

This bewildering variety makes it difficult to draw any clear conclusions about religion. However, one conclusion expressed almost universally is that religion is a force for good.

In nearly every land, religion is hailed as the noblest quest of the human spirit. Successful politicians usually belong to a major church and tell the faithful that their beliefs are the pillars of the nation. (Edward Gibbon wrote in *The Decline and Fall of the Roman Empire:* "The various modes of worship which prevailed in the Roman world were all considered by the people as equally true; by the philosophers as equally false; and by the magistrates as equally useful.")

Is religion a force for good? The evidence of history and the evidence of current events cast doubt on the truism. Nobel Peace Prize winner Elie Wiesel remarked: "When has religion ever been unifying? Religion has introduced many wars in this world, enough bloodshed and violence."

Philosopher Bertrand Russell wrote: "Religion is based . . . mainly upon fear . . fear of the mysterious, fear of defeat, fear of death. Fear is the parent of cruelty, and therefore it is no wonder if cruelty and religion have gone hand in hand. . . . My own view on religion is that of Lucretius. I regard it as a disease born of fear and as a source of untold misery to the human race."

Ernest Lefever, president of the Ethics and Public Policy Center in Washington, D.C., says religious combat is excessively cruel because "if you feel God is on your side, you can justify any atrocity."

Psychologist Albert Ellis wrote: "Religious fanaticism has clearly produced, and in all probability will continue to produce, enormous amounts of bickering, fighting, violence, bloodshed, homicide, feuds, wars, and genocide. For all its peace-inviting potential, therefore, arrant (not to mention arrogant) religiosity has led to immense individual and social harm by fomenting an incredible amount of anti-human and anti-humane aggression."

Even some devout believers are sickened by religion's record. Theologian Clark Williamson said of anti-Semitism:

"Of the many difficulties in writing about the treatment of Jews by Christians, not least is the problem of believability. That some things could have occurred seems scarcely credible. Yet they did. . . . We have seen the collusion of Christianity with pogrom and Holocaust. . . . What is the goodness of this world . . . when millions are killed by those baptized in the name of the Redeemer? . . . The immensity of human suffering and death inflicted on Jews for 1,500 years by some who called themselves Christian, and the apparent worthlessness to

Christians of the lives of those who did not convert to Christianity, fundamentally question Christian claims about the value of human life. . . . Christians have lost forever the credibility of their claim to a superior religion and a superior ethic."

In 1989, after the Ayatollah Khomeini decreed assassination for the "blaspheming" author Salman Rushdie, American newspaper columnist Leonard Larson wrote that it was part of "the ancient religious tradition of slaying the heretics and stamping out contrary beliefs." He said past popes guarded the purity of doctrines by using "the gibbet and the stake and other religious instruments of the day." The advent of modern weaponry means that "the devout can now bomb jet airliners out of the sky or dynamite women's care clinics or rain death on children, all with the serenity of serving their true God." Scholar Arthur Schlesinger Jr. observed in a 1989 speech:

"As a historian, I confess to a certain amusement when I hear the Judeo-Christian tradition praised as the source of our present-day concern for human rights; that is, for the valuable idea that all individuals everywhere are entitled to life, liberty, and the pursuit of happiness on this earth. In fact, the great religious ages were notable for their indifference to human rights in the contemporary sense. They were notorious not only for acquiescence in poverty, inequality, exploitation, and oppression, but also for enthusiastic justifications of slavery, persecution, abandonment of small children, torture, and genocide.

"During most of the history of the West . . . religion enshrined and vindicated hierarchy, authority, and inequality, and had no compunction about murdering heretics and blasphemers. Until the end of the 18th century, torture was normal investigative procedure in the Catholic church as well as in most European states . . .

"Human rights is not a religious idea. It is a secular idea, the product of the last four centuries of Western history. Tocqueville persuasively attributed the humanitarian ethic to the rise of the idea of equality. . . . It was the age of equality that brought about the disappearance of such religious appurtenances as the auto-da-fé and burning at the stake, the abolition of torture and of public executions, the emancipation of the slaves. . . . The basic human rights documents—the American Declaration of Independence and the French

222

Declaration of the Rights of Man—were written by political, not by religious, leaders."

It might be noted, sarcastically, that religion caused one development in human rights: Because victims were tortured in the Inquisition chambers and in the Star Chamber to make them "confess" heresy, political thinkers later devised the Fifth Amendment, which guarantees that no person shall be compelled to be a witness against himself.

In another area of human rights, many Christian clergymen advocated slavery. Historian Larry Hise notes in his book *Pro-Slavery* that ministers "wrote almost half of all defenses of slavery published in America." He listed 275 men of the cloth who used the Bible to prove that white people were entitled to own black people as work animals.

In Elizabethan England, a devoutly pious slaver, Sir John Hawkins, named his slave ships *Jesus, Angel,* and *Grace of God.* If any of the wretches chained below decks could understand their ship's name, they must have been bewildered indeed.

And the future human rights of many small boys were violated in Italy in the 1600s when they were surgically converted into silver-voiced castrati for the great church choirs.

Meanwhile, in today's world, the daily news endlessly reports savagery by religious combatants. "Muslim terrorists" and "Hindu assailants" and "Christian snipers" are standard headline phrases. The Santa Barbara Peace Resource Center in California said thirty-two wars were in progress around the globe in 1988, and twenty-five of them had "a significant ethnic, racial, or religious dimension." For example, Muslim Indonesia invaded the Catholic island nation of East Timor in 1975 and killed hundreds of thousands of residents during the next decade and a half. As for the multiple conflicts of the Middle East, theologian Martin Marty of the University of Chicago said: "Look at that situation for five minutes and you discover that behind the guns are scriptures."

Writer Amos Elon says religion and nationalism have become nearly synonymous in Jerusalem, a city where "one hates one's fellow man to the greater glory of God."

Is religion a force for good? This much is self-evident: Religion has a great potential for evil—and that potential has been realized thousands of times through the years.

There is plenty of non-religious horror in the world. In the killing fields of Cambodia, rural peasants slew millions of city dwellers, largely for economic reasons. In Latin America, right-wing death squads assassinate labor leaders and teachers for political reasons. In Burundi and Rwanda, the Tutsis (the tall ones) periodically massacre the Hutus (the short ones) for tribal reasons. Many different causes trigger the human instinct for slaughter.

Yet it's profoundly depressing that religion—supposedly the cure for human cruelty—often is just another basis for murder and madness.

BIBLIOGRAPHY

As far as can be ascertained, no previous book has surveyed the phenomenon of religious homicide in its entirety. Many books, however, have addressed specific aspects and historical occurrences. The following is a selected reading list, by topic.

Crusades

Billings, Malcolm. *The Cross and the Crescent.* Sterling Publishing, New York, 1988.

Bradford, Ernle. *The Sword and the Scimitar.* G. P. Putnam's Sons, New York, 1974.

Bridge, Antony. *The Crusades.* Franklin Watts, New York, 1980.

Dahmus, Joseph. *The Middle Ages.* Doubleday, Garden City, N.Y., 1968.

Finucane, Ronald. *Soldiers of the Faith*. St. Martin's Press, New York, 1983.

Gascoigne, Bamber. *The Christians*. William Morrow, New York, 1977.

Gillingham, John. *Richard the Lionheart*. Times Books, New York, 1978.

Lamb, Harold. *The Crusades*. Doubleday, Garden City, N.Y., 1930.

Mackay, Charles. *Extraordinary Popular Delusions and the Madness of Crowds*. London, 1841.

Oldenbourg, Zoe. *The Crusades*. Pantheon, New York, 1966.

Payne, Robert. *The Dream and the Tomb*. Stein & Day, New York, 1984.

Pernoud, Regine. *In the Steps of the Crusaders*. Hastings House, New York, 1959.

Setton, Kenneth. *A History of the Crusades*. University of Pennsylvania Press, Philadelphia, 1962.

Theis, Dan. *The Crescent and the Cross*. Thomas Nelson, Inc., Nashville, Tenn., 1978.

Thompson, Ernest Trice. *Through the Ages: A History of the Christian Church*. CLC Press, Richmond, Va., 1965.

Treece, Henry. *The Crusades*. Random House, New York, 1963.

Sacrifice

Burland, Cottie. *The Aztecs*. Orbis, London, 1975.

Campbell, Joseph. *The Mythic Image*. Princeton University Press, Princeton, N.J., 1974.

Fagan, Brian. *Clash of Cultures*. W. H. Freeman, New York, 1984.

Frazer, Sir James George. *The Golden Bough*. Macmillan, London, 1935.

Thomas, Paul. *Incredible India*. D. B. Taraporevala Sons, Bombay, 1966.

Killing Jews

Bratton, Fred. *The Crime of Christendom*. Beacon, Boston, 1969.

Eban, Abba. *Heritage: Civilization and the Jews*. Summit, New York, 1984.

Glassman, Samuel. *Epic of Survival: Twenty-five Centuries of Anti-Semitism*. Bloch Publishing, New York, 1980.

Grosser, Paul, and Edwin Halperin. *The Causes and Effects of Anti-Semitism*. Philosophical Library, New York, 1978.

Litvinoff, Barnet. *The Burning Bush: Anti-Semitism and World History*. E. P. Dutton, New York, 1988.

Parkes, James. *The Jew in the Medieval Community*. Hermon Press, New York, 1976.

Rubenstein, Richard. *After Auschwitz: Religion and the Origins of the Death Camps*. Bobbs-Merrill, Indianapolis, Ind., 1966.

Runes, Robert. *The Jew and the Cross*. Philosophical Library, New York, 1965.

———. *The War Against the Jew*. Philosophical Library, New York, 1968.

Williamson, Clark M. *Has God Rejected His People? Anti-Judaism in the Christian Church*. Abingdon, Nashville, Tenn., 1982.

Ziegler, Philip. *The Black Death*. John Day Co., New York, 1969.

Inquisition

Johnson, Paul. *A History of Christianity*. Atheneum, New York, 1976.

Kiekhefer, Richard. *Repression of Heresy in Medieval Germany*. University of Pennsylvania Press, Philadelphia, 1979.

Latourette, Kenneth. *A History of Christianity*. Harper & Row, New York, 1953.

Lea, Henry Charles. *A History of the Inquisition*. Macmillan, London, 1922.

Nigg, Walter. *The Heretics*. Alfred A. Knopf, New York, 1962.

Schevill, Ferdinand. *History of Florence*. Harper & Row, New York, 1936.

Van Loon, Hendrick. *Tolerance*. Liveright Publishing, New York, 1927.

Witch-Hunts

Hansen, Chadwick. *Witchcraft at Salem*. George Brazilier, New York, 1969.

Hart, Roger. *Witchcraft*. G. P. Putnam's Sons, New York, 1972.

Hueffer, Oliver. *The Book of Witches*. Rowman & Littlefield, Totowa, N.J., 1973.

Jong, Erica. *Witches*. Harry N. Abrams, Inc., New York, 1981.

Van Vuuren, Nancy. *The Subversion of Women, as Practiced by Churches, Witch-Hunters, and Other Sexists.* Westminster Press, Philadelphia, 1973.

Reformation

Chamberlain, E. R. *The Bad Popes.* Dial Press, New York, 1969.

Cowie, Leonard. *The Reformation.* G. P. Putnam's Sons, New York, 1970.

Daniel-Rops, Henry. *The Catholic Reformation.* E. P. Dutton, New York, 1962.

De Rosa, Peter. *Vicars of Christ: The Dark Side of the Papacy.* Crown Publishers, New York, 1988.

Dickens, A. G. *Reformation and Society in 16th Century Europe.* Thames & Hudson, London, 1966.

———. *The Counter Reformation.* Harcourt, Brace & World, London, 1969.

Foxe, John. *Foxe's Book of English Martyrs.* 1554 and 1564, reprinted by Word Books, Waco, Tex., 1981.

Grimm, Harold J. *The Reformation Era: 1500–1650.* Macmillan, New York, 1973.

Luyken, Jan. *Martyrs Mirror.* Holland, 1685.

Tuchman, Barbara. *The March of Folly.* Alfred A. Knopf, New York, 1984.

Zophy, Jonathan. *The Holy Roman Empire.* Greenwood Press, Westport, Conn., 1980.

Puritans

Hoffman, Edwin. *Pathways to Freedom.* Houghton Mifflin, Boston, 1964.

MacManus, Seumas. *The Story of the Irish Race.* Devin-Adair Co., Old Greenwich, Conn., 1921.

Enlightenment

Ayer, A. J. *Thomas Paine.* Atheneum, New York, 1988.

Goll, Yvan. *The Torch of Freedom.* Farrar & Rinehart, New York, 1943.

Sepoy Mutiny

Morris, James. *Heaven's Command.* Harvest/HBJ, New York and London, 1973.

Baha'is

Sears, William. *A Cry from the Heart: The Baha'is in Iran.* George Ronald, Oxford, England, 1982.

Armenia

Feigl, Erich. *A Myth of Terror.* Edition Zeitgeschichte, Salzburg, 1986.

Oke, Mim Kemal. *The Armenian Question, 1914–1923*. K.
    Rustem & Brother, London, 1988.
Sonyel, Salahi. *The Ottoman Armenians*. K. Rustem &
    Brother, London, 1987.

Muslim Gore

Roberts, D. S. *Islam*. Harper & Row, New York, 1981.
Urban, Mark. *War in Afghanistan*. St. Martin's Press, New
    York.
Wright, Robin. *Sacred Rage: The Wrath of Militant Islam*.
    Simon & Schuster, New York, 1985.

Force for Good?

Russell, Bertrand. *Why I Am Not a Christian*. 1927,
    reprinted by Simon & Schuster, New York, 1957.
Schlesinger, Arthur, Jr. Lecture at Brown University on
    the inauguration of Vartan Gregorian as president,
    1989.